THE ARCH
OF DESIRE

THE ARCH

OF DESIRE

AN EROTIC NOVEL

Vicente Muñoz Puelles

Translated from the Spanish by Kristina Cordero

Grove Press / *New York*

Originally published in Spanish under the title *La curvatura
del empeine* by Tusquets Editores, Barcelona.

Published simultaneously in Canada
Printed in the United States of America

FIRST EDITION

Library of Congress Cataloging-in-Publication Data

Muñoz Puelles, Vicente.
   [Curvatura del empeine. English]
   The arch of desire : an erotic novel / Vicente Muñoz Puelles ; translated
from the Spanish by Kristina Cordero.— 1st ed.
     p. cm.
   ISBN 0-8021-3969-8
   1. Molinier, Pierre, 1900–1976—Fiction.   I. Cordero, Kristina.
II. Title.
PQ6663.U485 C8713 2003
863'.64—dc21

                                             2002035447

Grove Press
841 Broadway
New York, NY 10003

03 04 05 06 10 9 8 7 6 5 4 3 2 1

Contents

Contents

THE ARCH
OF DESIRE

I

The Woman Who Rode
Away on Horseback

The sight of your foot is disturbing me.
—Gustave Flaubert, *The Sentimental Education*

Many years before I was born, my father's first wife would let the château dogs loose as a way of protecting herself against some unknown intruder that was stalking her, intent upon infiltrating her dream life. That, at least, was the story Anne-Marie told my sister Muriel and me. Anne-Marie had been the maidservant of my father's first wife, and of my mother later on. She told us the story in Domaine de Chevalier, a country building with two identical towers that still stands against the backdrop of a vast open field filled with vineyards and surrounded by a thicket of pine trees in the district of Graves, to the south of Bordeaux. By the time we heard the story, the lovely Polish woman had long since died, but we knew her image well from all the photographs and paintings in the château. And Muriel was the living reflection of that image, which seemed more real to us than many of the people we saw every day, such as the château workers and even Anne-Marie.

"Your father worshipped her," the maidservant would often recall wistfully.

Unlike Muriel, who was the Polish woman's daughter and three years my senior, I would grow jealous of that mythical woman every time Anne-Marie said that. And although my mother had clearly taken her place in my father's heart, the Polish woman's alluring ghost continued to roam through the garden, linger in the immense armoire, and occasionally lean out from the second-floor windows. One afternoon, I thought I saw her amid the shadows of the wine press, where the naked men would crush the grapes in the giant oak barrels. It was a fleeting, feminine apparition that danced through my imagination long before I ever laid eyes on her image, and it always vanished the moment I would try to seize hold of it. Muriel claimed not to sense this presence and refused to believe it existed at all, but whenever I would feel the Polish woman's ghost hovering nearby, Muriel would inevitably begin to chatter away nervously, or she would bend down to pick something off the floor as if trying to distract me.

Anne-Marie told us my father had discovered that woman with the great big eyes one day as he was walking along the banks of the Seine. At first he had been drawn to her exotic clothes—out-of-the-ordinary in France at the time, and out-of-season as well—but he was equally captivated by the odd way she walked: elevated, almost on tiptoe, teetering upon her high heels. And he was captivated, too, by the way she kept turning around, as if to check whether someone was following her.

The details of that first rendezvous fed my fantasy life during a great deal of my childhood and adolescence. The Polish woman herself had told the story to Anne-Marie, who then passed it down to us, telling us how my father had offered this strange woman protection and aid in a moment of selfless gallantry. My childish imagination staged the encounter in its own simplistic way: my father would surprise her as she gazed out over the river, filled with nostalgia and longing, and then he would jump in after her to rescue her from drowning. He saved her that day, delaying a suicide that, in the end, was inevitable, because she was poor and she was alone. He took her to her hotel, where he removed her soaked clothes and was spellbound by a beauty which I could only scarcely imagine in all my youthful inexperience.

In other, later versions of the story, I saw her wearing smooth white leather gloves with a long line of backstitching on the underside. My father would remove them slowly, expertly, a gesture that was shockingly intimate to her—it felt as if he were removing her embroidered knickers. The mysterious foreign woman's cheeks would grow hot as he kissed her bare fingers one by one, and then her soft palms; here and there, in little fleeting instants, she could feel the tip of his tongue making contact with her skin. His kisses would grow bolder, traveling across her forehead, her wide cheekbones, her thick lips, and her strong swan's neck. As if caught in a dream, she would feel my father's fingers untying her corset, and caressing her ardent breasts, as her ginger-colored nipples grew abundant and hard.

As my father would whisper sweet words in her ear, he would unfasten the belt of her dress, explore the closures that ran up her back, unbutton the wide cuffs of her blouse, and then, with her assistance, pull her dress up and her petticoats down. At the gentle fluttering of his fingers, her feminine crevice would prepare for him, growing soft and warm. Firmly on the road to ecstasy, she would take his proud member in her hands—at this moment of my fantasy, I reached for my own as well—and she would guide it inside her luscious opening. His thighs tense, my father would kneel down on the bed as his hands gripped her ankles. He would shift her body up a bit, settling into an oddly vertical position, high enough so that as he plunged into her, he could watch himself making love to her.

"Oh, how lovely," the foreign woman would sigh in a tremulous voice, as my father's insistent arrow dug deeper and deeper inside of her, pounding back and forth like the piston of a steam engine or the tip of an immense, thick syringe.

"Ohh, ohh," I would moan, and then I would rise up on the tips of my toes as pearly spurts of rain fell down from my shuddering member, spouting out into midair, in search of that elusive ghost.

My father was an extraordinarily sensual man, just as I am, and I think it was that odd, inaccessible aura that made him fall in love with the Polish émigré—an aura another man might have perceived as a sign of madness. In any event, he took care of her, he doted on her, and he married her, giving her his title and his name. She, however, never revealed to him the mystery of her arrival in France, and she always refused to discuss her past with him. He could enjoy the myriad pleasures of her warm, welcoming belly beneath his own, and her tender breasts pressing against his chest, and the intimate caresses that brought him such ecstasy, but she never told her secret to him, and for that reason she would always remain elusive. But it seemed he knew that their happiness could only be temporary—that someone, someday, would come from far away and take her from him.

After two years of married life, Muriel was born, and shortly thereafter the Polish woman disappeared. They found her body, naked and dead, somewhere near the ocean. She had taken one of the horses from the stables and galloped through the rain all night long until she fell while trying to jump a fence. Her neck was broken. How could she have gone so far without being seen by anyone? Why did she ride in the nude? Where had she been going? Nobody knew. The château dogs had also disappeared that night, never to return, said Anne-Marie.

The rumors surrounding her death still hadn't fully subsided when my father was married again, this time to a very young woman from Bordeaux—my mother. It seemed that he still yearned for the Polish woman and was still tormented by the fact that he had never truly understood her. Whenever he spoke of her, he would always focus on the most trivial, insignificant details— always the same details—and always avoiding the two things we *really* wanted to know: whether he thought she had truly loved him and whether it was true that she had lived beneath a kind of dark cloud, plagued by constant fears. My father saved a number of her things and hid them away in one of his desk drawers: a shiny lock of hair, a tiny bottle filled with fingernail clippings, a pair of patent leather slippers with a feather in the crown, and a bottle of perfume, Saoko, which on more than one occasion we caught him sniffing with a faraway expression on his face, oblivious to the possibility that anyone might be watching him.

I was ten years old then, and my mental montages of that first encounter between my father and the Polish woman were still a long way from serving as a prelude to my own particular pleasures. But one night, I was stirred awake by the vision of a succulent, open vulva rubbing back and forth against the mane and bare back of a galloping horse, and for the first time ever I ejaculated. The horse's hooves would pound against the earth in rhythm with each spurt of ecstasy, and my linen nightshirt would grow slowly hot and moist.

II

The Champagne-Colored Corset

In the afternoons at l'Eau Blanche, the drainage canal that skirted the southern edge of our vineyards, the loons would carry out their complicated courtship rituals during the mating season. With their crests fully erect, they would rise up, breast against breast, then separate. Then they would lunge toward one another above the water at great speed, their necks arched backward though never touching, and their wings would meet in midair. From there, they would plunge into the water together, at exactly the same moment, to conclude what Muriel and I imagined was an underwater ritual whose finale was not meant for our eyes. Other birds would mate noisily in the reed beds or upon the rotting bed of water lilies. There was another species—a duck, or perhaps it was a teal—that gasped and sighed just as humans did. We never actually saw these animals, but we knew they had to be birds because whenever we approached them they would make their escape through the tall reeds and we could hear the rustling and the scandalized flapping of wings preparing for flight.

Great mansions can be grand and luxurious places, but they can be so very cold as well. Ours, which was modest compared to others in the châteaux region, was the kind of mansion that aroused the five senses, rigorously testing our faculties. The fragrance of wine permeated everything—the odor of fermentation, the simple smell of wine made from young grapes, the pungent scent of strong, full-bodied wine, the complex aromas of age. The largest building, used as a warehouse, was an immense, partially subterranean shed connected to another building where the wine was distilled and fermented. The mansion we lived in was a labyrinth of staircases, passageways, and corridors that led from one room to the next, the rather haphazard result of a succession of building additions. There were hidden doorways that led to secret bedrooms and elaborately mirrored doors that opened onto giant armoires built against the brick walls behind. The house was filled with hidden corners, planters with tall, willowy ferns, and lamps, vases, and furniture of undulating, organic shapes and contours.

On special occasions, which were usually associated with the wine harvest or some other holiday, my parents would invite their friends to spend the night, and Muriel and I would steal away from our bedrooms to listen to the sound of the beds creaking. Around midnight, or sometimes in the early afternoon hours, the noise would grow more and more insistent, as would the moans, occasionally culminating in screams, of the impassioned couples in question. Occasionally the various love battles would be waged in a kind of symphony, and the sounds would climb to a crescendo until the entire house seemed to tremble beneath their force. The identical towers would sway to and fro, the chandeliers would rock back and forth, the ghost of the Polish woman would suddenly come alive, and the very air would shake, crying out loud, "Yes! Yes! Do it again, faster, faster!" In the mornings, I would inspect the abandoned trays lying outside the closed bedroom doors, in search of lipstick traces on the rims of the glasses that had been used for nighttime toasts, and I would get drunk as I curled my lips around them and drank down their remains. There was no running water in those days, and the house servants would fill the tubs with water for baths. Sometimes Muriel and I would press our noses against the washroom doors to catch a whiff of that aromatic blend of creams, perfumes, and faint scents released by those pampered bodies.

One day, as I walked past the washing room, a champagne-colored corset caught my eye. That night, in my bed, I conjured up its dimensions and brilliant designs in my mind. Barefoot, with an oil lamp in my hand and my heart on tenterhooks, I slid down the labyrinthine halls into the bowels of the great house. The door to the washing room was locked. After locating the keys, I slowly opened the door, fearful that the corset would be gone. Once inside, I allowed myself a deep sigh of pent-up anxiety as I clung to the silken bodice. The neckline was dotted with bits of appliquéd lace, and four elastic straps hung down from the bottom, where one would attach a pair of stockings. The bottom hem had a triangular cut, which probably was intended to stretch down to the navel. I finished off my treasure trove with a few *eau-de-nil* colored petticoats and a pair of fishnet stockings I found in another basket. To avoid being caught in possession of this stolen finery, I snuffed out the oil lamp and crept back upstairs in darkness, losing my way and nearly ending up in Muriel's bedroom.

Once back in my own room, I played various different games with my spoils: I stuffed my pillow into the corset, bundled up my vigorous member in the petticoats, and with one of the fishnet stockings wrapped around my hand, I began to massage my throbbing rod. The garments were freshly washed, but my nose, highly attuned from years of experience with our wines, perceived several distinct aromatic sources. In the corset, for example, I noted a hint of amber which told me it belonged to my mother. Finally, desperate to recreate a feminine figure who could provide me with the pleasure I so desired, I placed the items on the floor, each one in its proper position relative to the others, with the elastic straps fastened to the stockings. Then, as I began to envision a pair of firm breasts, opulent buttocks, and a pair of feet that stretched out to fill the fine fishnet stockings all the way through to the toes, the blood came rushing into my head, my body began to tremble with fury, and I spilled my abundant riches from bottom to top and then from top to bottom upon that imaginary woman who was like the photographic negative of a real woman made of flesh and blood. Then I fell to the floor, as if hit by a thunderbolt. Even now, so many years later, after a life marked by a truly myriad array of orgasms, I still recall the violence of that release.

In due time, my breathing returned to normal. I got up and began to clean the stains off the undergarments with the water in my washbasin. From my experience with bedsheets I knew that semen often seemed to wash off easily at first, but once it dried it would leave a stiff, crystalline stain like the kind made by a drop of wax. I also knew that applying soap to specific spots only contributed to the hardening process. With this in mind, I simply wet the sticky trail of semen with water, and rubbed it away with a towel. As my hands made contact with the molded cups of the corset, I began to grow aroused again. I reassembled the figure, this time on the bed, and another offering quickly came bubbling out from my emboldened spout—briefer than before, but just as intense. As my sperm spilled out, the large tiles with flower designs acquired a sheen that was like a brilliant coat of varnish.

I folded the various negligees and put them back in the washing room. But this little nocturnal adventure was as romantic as any midnight escape I could envision with a real woman, and so I repeated it on several occasions. I never found the champagne-colored corset again, but I did find other things: rose- and tea-colored peignoirs, myrtle-green bustiers, hyacinth-blue bustiers, embroidered knickers, and other kinds of splendid little trifles—precursors to modern lingerie, I suppose, though infinitely more subtle and intriguing. I occasionally came upon items that belonged to some female guest, but the most thrilling, diaphanous, and alluring pieces were always the ones that belonged to my mother.

One night I found that the key to the washing room was not in its usual spot. Naturally I was perplexed by this turn of events, and I could not figure out why the key had moved. I had grown so accustomed to fondling and toying with those feminine playthings—they were like pieces of a great puzzle to me—that the prospect of masturbating without them was utterly unexciting. So I felt tremendously relieved when, some time later, the key was returned to its usual spot. On my bedroom floor, I spread out the sumptuous array of feminine frippery— an intoxicating bustier and negligee, a pair of the darkest black stockings—and my little friend rose up eagerly, even before I began to stroke it. At some point in all this, I had added a new twist to the ritual: I would murmur a litany of female names that would come pouring into my head—names which had no relation to any women I actually knew.

"Sophie . . . , Justine . . . , Justine . . . , Nicole . . . , Nicole . . . ," I cried out breathlessly.

That same night, just when I could no longer control the wave that was threatening to flood the proverbial dam, the door opened and Anne-Marie entered the room. In the frenzy of my desire, I had forgotten to lock the door. Flustered and dumbstruck, I turned to face her, though I was powerless to stop the convulsive waves of ecstasy that now shuddered through my body.

"Nicole . . . Anne-Marie! Anne-Marie!" I muttered with clenched teeth, as I came fiercely.

"Oh, Sir!" she exclaimed, unable to take her eyes off my subsiding erection. "This explains so many things, Monsieur Pierre."

"This . . . this is not what it seems, Anne-Marie," I stammered.

"But, Monsieur Pierre, you don't have to apologize. At your age, why this is quite normal . . . All the women in this house have seen how your eyes linger on all the ladies' legs. But if you had only told me what you were doing with your mother's clothes, I wouldn't have worried so, and I would have thought of some way for you to satisfy yourself without making me wash and iron so much. Come here, now."

Gently tugging at my limp penis, she drew me toward the washbasin and washed and dried me, treating me like the little boy I was.

"You won't say anything to my mother, will you?"

"No, but you must promise me that from now on you'll behave yourself and you won't make me work so hard."

"I promise."

"May I ask a slightly indiscreet question, Monsieur Pierre?"

"Of course you may, Anne-Marie."

"Everyone knows that boys relieve their sexual tension with their hands. Of course, you are only eleven years old, which is a bit early. Have you been playing with your little violin for very long?"

"I don't quite know, to be honest. Not very long, I don't think. First I began having . . . dreams, at night, and then I found I could make it happen myself, at any time of the day."

"And you use these clothes because it feels nicer?"

"Yes. The clothes help me imagine what I would do with a woman."

"Hmmm . . . so much wasted energy!"

Anne-Marie's fingers continued touching and caressing my soft penis, which began to grow stiff. Without taking her eyes off me, she went over to the door, closed the latch, and lowered the light in the oil lamp. Then she gathered up the clothes, placed them on a chair, and began to play with my stiff member once again.

"How quickly you've regained your potency, Monsieur Pierre. It's quite impressive. The tip is all purple now, and the little eye has opened up again. Would you like me to help?"

"I'd like that very much."

"Put your hand between my legs."

I obeyed gratefully. My hand slid beneath the skirt of her uniform and patted the smooth surface of her inner thighs. Anne-Marie wore nothing under the skirt, and so I easily found my way toward the thick mat of curly hair.

I caressed it, thrilled by the feeling of her thick, partially opened lips. From the garden outside, I could hear the wry sound of an owl's cry.

"Does that feel good?" Anne-Marie asked me sweetly.

"Oh yes, so good. It's so warm, so wet . . ."

With her free hand, she took my wrist and guided it downward until I felt a tiny button beneath the tip of my finger.

"This is the most important spot," she whispered. "Stroke it slowly and then go down, like this, and then stroke it again after making a little circle with your fingers. Good, good! You're learning very quickly."

Without letting go of my rigid staff, Anne-Marie began to quiver and sigh. A watery liquid trickled down from her insides, wetting my fingers. I was filled with pride at the idea that I could be the source of such pleasure.

"Oh, there, there!" she murmured. "Yes, yes!"

Her belly trembled, and she briefly, suddenly arched her back. For a few moments, she rested the weight of her body on her heels, lost in the throes of violent spasms and moans—an orgasm that was the spark that ignited my own. Anne-Marie made me turn around a bit, so that I wouldn't ejaculate on her, and with peerless instinct and acuity she administered the coup de grace, that is, the final few thrusts I needed.

"Ahh . . . ahh!" I moaned in full delirium, held captive by the iron grip of her hand.

Before leaving me, she washed and dried me once again, and tucked me into bed. Then she gathered up the clothing that lay on the chair and she turned back to look at me as her hand rested on the latch to the door.

"You are a most robust boy, Monsieur Pierre. When you grow up, you will make many, many women happy."

III

The Carved Ivory Tusk

From then on, Anne-Marie's secret, postmidnight visits became the high point of my day. Naked under the sheets and blanket, I would wait for her with the impatient erection of a passionate, eager young boy. I always felt tempted to feign sleep and pretend that my very obvious erection was involuntary, as a way of inspiring her awe and admiration. But I never actually did it, fearing her respect for my sleeping figure would overcome her lust and she would leave the room without catching on to the ruse. And so, as she entered the room, I would sit up and proudly display my turgid weapon, just like the images I had seen of a cocksure Dionysius admiring his own phallus. Anne-Marie would match my boldness, guiding me toward the little bud hidden beneath her mat of curls, encouraging me to caress it and delve into her warm, sweet lips as she took hold of my penis, which would be pulsating insistently by this time—and she would begin to massage it back and forth.

Whenever I was the first to reach orgasm—which was almost always—she would stop, patiently wipe away the traces of my youthful passion, then turn my attention to her own pleasure. The contemplation of her ecstasy always revived my own desire. Then she would make me lie down on the bed and, eluding my embrace, she would settle down to face my tremulous member. She would begin to manipulate it once again, lying in wait for my second offering, to which she inevitably reacted with an odd kind of surprise.

"Oh!" she would exclaim. "What a fascinating little pistol you have, Monsieur Pierre! Always ready to fire away one more time."

I would release everything I had inside me, and then she would claim fatigue, but if I insisted enough, she would let me play another game with her little jewels. She would stand up, her skirt pushed up above her knees, and I would sit on the edge of the bed facing her. Easing my fingers into her creamy pink crevice I would make her anxious button tremble with pleasure, just as she had instructed me. The vision of her ecstasy was so exhilarating that I wished I could make it last for hours. I almost thought I could hear a little cry escape from between her legs, a sound that, to me, was the very voice of her orgasm. And as I tried hard to hold her back, she would playfully admonish me, "Come now, haven't you had enough already? You're insatiable!"

"Oh, but I want you so much . . . and if you don't help me I'll have to do it myself and then I'll make a terrible mess of the bedsheets . . ."

Although almost invariably she would ignore my pleas, occasionally she would give in and we would satisfy each other for a third time.

One thing was odd: her mouth held little fascination for me. I had kissed a few girls, including my sister, to no great avail, and so I thought of kissing as more a sign of affection than of pleasure. I don't remember ever having kissed Anne-Marie, and I can't even remember her face very clearly, but the lengthy succession of genital landscapes that I have contemplated throughout my life in no way dims my memory of those tender folds of flesh beneath the copper-colored curls decorating her pubis.

Sensual pleasure, which heightens with time and practice, also comes alive with change. Sometimes I would ask her to lie down with me in bed and let me look at her breasts or caress them as I masturbated, and other times I would ask if I could kneel before her open thighs and penetrate that smooth threshold with my member. But she always said no, claiming that the simplicity of our lovemaking ritual was what made her feel safer. In reality, it didn't matter much to me, because in questions of the flesh two people can never be perfectly calibrated, especially when one person is young and possessed by such blinding desire.

Aware that she had been with the same boyfriend for a long time, one night I asked her if she was a virgin.

"Of course I'm a virgin! What kind of girl do you think I am?" she asked, shocked. "A girl is a virgin until she lets a man enter her with his member, and I've only allowed fingers to penetrate me. And don't think I haven't been tempted. If someone really wanted to . . ."

With her boyfriend, she explained, she did exactly what she did with me: mutual masturbation. The only difference was that he liked her to milk him quickly, in rapid-fire motion. It was always brief, she said, and he was so unconcerned with her pleasure that he often left her unsatisfied. What she liked about me was that she could prolong my climaxes indefinitely, as if drawing out every last bit of pleasure. But it was more than that: I seemed to enjoy fondling her almost as much as I enjoyed what she did to me.

I also asked her if my prick was small compared with her boyfriend's.

"No, Monsieur Pierre, that is where you are mistaken," she replied. "Marcel's is thicker, but yours is almost as long, and with all this exercise yours will surely continue to grow as time goes by. And yours is more elegant as well. With all those veins and bulges, and that fine point at the tip, it makes me think of one of those carved ivory tusks that they sell in the antique shops."

Sometimes she would tell me about the Polish woman, for whom she began to work at a very young age. In a tremulous voice that made me wonder if she had fallen in love with her, Anne-Marie would describe her silken skin, her shapely thighs, and her perfect feet.

I grew so accustomed to her presence in my bedroom that once, when she went to Agen to visit her family for three days, I missed her terribly and scolded her for having left me when she returned. That was when she handed me a flesh-colored stocking and said, "When I'm away, you can use this in place of me."

"What shall I do with it?"

"Well . . . two things come to mind."

We tried both. The first consisted of suspending the stocking between my two hands with my penis resting on top, rubbing it back and forth as you would two sticks to start a fire. She demonstrated the second technique by taking the stocking and making a tight knot around my penis: then I was to raise it up toward my belly and then lower it, as if playing with a yo-yo. Both methods proved effective and eminently worthy of my impassioned tribute.

One night, her face more flushed than usual, she announced that she was pregnant. I was quite moved by this bit of news, but wasted no time in arguing that, as far as I could see, I wasn't the cause.

"Don't worry, Monsieur Pierre," she said sweetly. "Of course it's not yours. Although I do consider you somewhat accountable, because your insistence was what finally made me give in to Marcel, and give him the thing that I always refused you."

She told me that they were to be married, and that she was happy, for she was over thirty years old and her boyfriend would take that decisive step now that she was pregnant.

I knew then that I had lost her forever. Seeing me cry like a little child whose toys have just been stolen, she gave me one final gift: at last, she allowed me to look at her breasts and place a kiss on each of the warm, alabaster globes decorated by a delicate trail of tiny blue blood vessels.

"You're going too far," she murmured flirtatiously, speaking to me in the familiar for the first time as I watched her nipples grow hard inside the halo of their areolas.

I masturbated one last time with her, and then she was gone. For a long time afterward, I would console myself by caressing my body with her empty stocking, but I soon realized that I had the perfect person with whom to complete my initiation: my sister.

IV

The Scar

When a very young boy becomes frightened and crawls toward his mother as fast as he can, is it not true that her shoe and the lower part of her leg are the first things he touches and clings to in order to feel safe again? Is it possible that I have lived my life beneath the twin signs of the high heel and the curving arch of a woman's foot as the result of my need to cling to that firm, ever-elusive appendage?

As Anne-Marie, my mother, and countless women who passed through our house knew that from a very young age I have always been drawn to the legs of women—those exquisitely shaped, disarmingly symmetrical forms. My mother had a weakness for shoes, and although many people insist that such early recollections are nonsense, I have no trouble at all going back almost seventy years, even though I am now seventy-six. I can still see myself sitting inside her closet among her many indulgences, inhaling the familiar scents of talcum powder and fine, pliant leather. Not all her fetishes were made of leather: some were satin, some were velvet or brocade, some were decorated with little buckles and bows, while others were bedecked with shiny black feathers that curled up toward the ankle.

I adored watching my mother step into her stockings, which she owned in every color, and I would watch, rapt, as she adjusted the darts, dots, or floral designs that ran up toward her calves and disappeared into dizzying heights. Sometimes, once they were properly fixed in place, she would cross her legs and invite me to play horse with them. She would hold me for a bit, balancing me on her shin, with my hands resting upon the convex curve of her knee. She would eventually let me go, but not before awakening emotions that I would be unable to banish for a long time.

When women would come to the house to visit, I would slide under the tables and, half hidden by the tablecloths, catch stolen glimpses of shoes, ankles, and maybe a hint of calves, as we were then in the era of long skirts. Occasionally, I would allow my hands to brush against those objects I so worshipped, those intimate places that seduced me so, and I was often amused to see that the women I fancied the most almost never protested when they realized it was a child doing those things to them, and they would usually allow me to continue doing whatever I wished. I grew bolder and bolder, and one woman even allowed me to remove her shoe under the table, and from a short lace-up boot I would extract a warm, slightly swollen foot from beneath a tight black leather tongue, nestled inside a thin silk stocking.

When I was given my own bedroom, each night I would ask my mother for one of her shoes and I would fall asleep gazing at it. My sister's taunts eventually made me give them up, but when Anne-Marie left, I felt the need to have them close again. The problem was that now, I didn't dare ask my mother for them.

One afternoon I went to see Muriel in her room. She was sitting at her dressing table, getting ready for dinner, her legs peeking out from her half-open robe. I felt a slight rumble inside of me and at that instant she became something terribly, terribly desirable, no longer the sister I was forced to endure.

Aware of the effect she'd had on me, she watched me with a little smile on her lips. Taking off her robe, she strode toward me in her petticoats. She had a muscular back, small, firm breasts, and a scar under her chin from when she had fallen down a flight of stairs as a little girl, though it was not particularly noticeable when you looked at her. She wore a pair of high heels that my father had given her for her fifteenth birthday. As she walked, her stocking-clad heel rose and fell to the floor with such an insistent click that I immediately became erect. I quickly sat down in a large, upholstered chair decorated with a scene from the fable of the fox and the grapes. I crossed my legs.

"All you men are so lecherous," Muriel observed shrewdly. By now she had clearly noticed the prominent bulge that throbbed beneath my pants. "All it takes is a bit of skin and there you go, drooling away."

"But isn't that exactly what you women try to provoke?" I retorted, in an attempt to challenge her like an adult would.

She turned halfway around, boldly placed herself directly in front of the chair that I had just sat down in, and lifted up her petticoats. She wore nothing underneath, and I caught a glimpse of a tiny mound of Venus protected by a little thicket.

"Do you think my legs are pretty?"

"They're magnificent."

"Do you like them more than Anne-Marie's?" she asked, with a hint of petulance.

"What makes you ask me that?"

One night, as it turned out, she had become intrigued by the moans emanating from my bedroom and climbed up the Italian aspen tree outside my window, the same tree in whose branches we had often played as children, where I used to watch the changing shadow cast by the house at sunset. Sitting up there, she had caught me with Anne-Marie during one of our evening encounters. To my shock, she recounted a few irrefutable details.

"The thing that surprised me the most," she said, "was how dedicated Anne-Marie was. You must feel very alone now."

She also bragged about climbing up into the branches of a giant oak tree and spying on our parents, who slept at the other end of the house.

"Now that it's summertime," she said, "they've become quite careless, and they always leave the balcony door open."

"Don't they turn out the light?"

She shook her head no, and looked into my eyes insistently, trying to gauge the effect of this revelation.

"You know what else? Your mother sucks off my father every night."

Satisfied by the astonished expression that must have come across my face, Muriel removed her petticoats and separated her legs. I sighed, and my sigh became a moan when my sister, determined to shock me, placed a finger in her mouth, savoring it as she licked it wet. Then she began to caress her tender opening surrounded by blond ringlets, which was now exactly level with my eyes. I breathed in a sweet fragrance, much more delicate than Anne-Marie's. Little by little the finger went further and further in, with ever-increasing determination, and the pink lips slowly spread apart to reveal a softer-hued hooded button.

"It feels so good!" she exclaimed wantonly. "I love to have you watching me."

With her free hand she massaged a breast, and I felt a wave of delight each time her belly rippled. My breath burned through me as Muriel took off one of her slippers and planted the bottom of her foot on the most sensitive part of my body.

"Even through your trousers I can feel you, hard and strong," she said.

That one single compliment conquered me completely. I didn't know what was more exciting: the sight of her arch hovering dangerously near, with those tiny lacquered toes hidden beneath her stocking, or her persistent massaging of my penis.

"Take it out already, Pierre," she ordered me. "I want to see the thing that so captivated Anne-Marie."

She rested her foot on the inside of my thigh, so that I could remove my undershorts, but my rod was so swollen by then that my clumsy manipulation only accelerated the process. From my contorted face, Muriel could see that I wouldn't be able to remove it in time, and so she put her foot on my groin, and rubbed her heel around and around. I clenched my teeth to keep from screaming as my sputtering member ejaculated onto my sister.

My rhythmic movements produced an instant response. She placed both hands between her thighs, separated her orchid's petals, and began to caress herself in a frenzy. Her entire body contracted in a spasm of pleasure that prolonged my own, and the violet-toned scar beneath her chin grew bright red, as if threatening to burst wide open.

V

The Snail's Trace

My erotic relationship with Muriel evolved much more smoothly than my relationship with Anne-Marie because it blossomed in an atmosphere of familiarity and companionship. In addition, my sister had a much more varied carnal repertoire, and she never missed an opportunity to enrich her palette of experiences. I, however, was so absorbed in my own fantasies that I scarcely even realized that she was carrying out various other romantic adventures right before my eyes. We attended different private schools in Léognan, and we would always return together but she always seemed to lag behind, luring some boy on a walk along l'Eau Blanche or through the vineyards.

What she liked best, she would tell me, was making her boyfriend of the moment lie down on his back with his penis erect. Then she would move it back and forth above him until he reached orgasm, never allowing him to penetrate her. One recent afternoon, however, she found herself in a bit of a jam. The young man in question had either been unable or unwilling to control himself and at the height of his ecstasy he tried to introduce his rose-colored scepter into my sister's warm, welcoming nest. Muriel, who had been enjoying herself tremendously, had quite a time summoning the necessary strength, first to push him off her and then to hit him with a rock. The frustrated lover, with his head bandaged up, told everyone that the men from a nearby town had gotten together to beat him up.

After observing a few of my nocturnal encounters with Anne-Marie, Muriel had begun to consider my possible aptitude as a lover, but she hadn't wanted to make a move until the day I visited her in her bedroom, when she tested the intensity of my appetite. Well aware that her brother would be far easier to control than any other man, she finally decided to make me her fortunate disciple.

The château library, which dated back to the days of my great-grandparents, was at least partially responsible for Muriel's sexual precociousness. Our parents had never forbidden me to take any volume from the stacks, but I was a student at the Christian Brothers' school, founded in the seventeenth century by Jean-Baptiste de la Salle, and had simply assumed that those solemn-looking volumes could only contain boring passages filled with strict, formalistic lessons. And so I looked upon her with skepticism when, with a devilish gleam in her eyes, she handed me an old copy of the Marquis de Sade's *Philosophy in the Bedroom* and challenged me to read it.

I had only read a few pages but by the time the libertine Dolmancé proclaimed that "the imagination is the spur of delights," I was already hard as a rock. Barely ten

or twelve lines farther along, I found Madame de Saint-
Ange declaring that "what is of the filthiest, the most
infamous, the most forbidden, 'tis that which best rouses
the intellect . . . 'tis that which always causes us most
deliciously to discharge." My sister studied me intently
as I read, as if I were a pianist and she were there to turn
the pages of the score. That was when she took hold of
my penis and began to massage it accordingly. Caught
in a blinding wave of rapture, I was unable to push the
book away in time, and a few white drops fell upon it and
languidly slid across the pages.

Muriel was wise to initiate me with *Philosophy in the
Bedroom,* an accelerated course in the ways of the libertine, and under its spell I came to believe that the pur-
suit of one's pleasure was the very most important thing
in the world. At that tender age I yearned to say the words
of Madame de Saint-Ange: "I have deposited five hundred *louis* with a notary, and the purse will belong to any
individual, whomsoever he be, who can teach me a passion I am ignorant of now, and who can plunge me into
an ecstasy I have not yet enjoyed."

Each night, as the servants and other adults in the
house went to sleep or engaged in the delights of Venus
and Priapo, my sister and I practiced our own techniques.
Inspired by both my own predilections and de Sade's
hearty recommendation, my most fervent desire was to
lick her cunt. Luck was on my side: despite the fact that
she had been standing and I had been seated for our first
encounter together, Muriel hardly objected to letting our

passions run free in bed, and in fact she was the one who wrestled me down onto the mattress.

Every vulva is unique, and responds in its own unique manner. Perhaps that, and our condition as mortal beings, are the only real truths known to man. Muriel's vulva was what the Latins referred to as *vulva fragans:* thick outer lips protected by a delicious blond thicket, with fleshy interior lips and a tiny, perpetually lubricated button.

As I bent down between her legs for the first time, my sister's pelvis arched upward. I gently licked her intimate little cave, my tongue following the circles that Anne-Marie had taught me to trace with my finger, just barely grazing the clitoris with my upper lip. Muriel sighed, but she was distracted. She asked me to sink my fingers into her vagina and explore it, as I continued licking her resplendent button. This aroused her even more, and her entire body began to tremble with pleasure. Seized by a sudden inspiration, I gently introduced my thumb into her anus. My sister began to moan as she dug her fingernails into my shoulders.

"Oh, Pierre," she exclaimed between gasps, "that's what I want! Do it!"

Emboldened by her command, I changed the direction of my caresses. I took her clitoris between my index finger and thumb as my tongue explored her ass and glided into her rosy crevice. My sister's hips began to shake violently, her nails dug deeper into the skin of my shoulders, and a prolonged wave of pleasure rocked through her body. For an instant I imagined that I was my father and she was the beautiful Polish woman.

"Now I know I can trust you," Muriel confided to me afterward as I lay on my back with my penis erect. She straddled me and began to administer her preferred treatment.

"I'm not so sure," I replied, raising my hand to my shoulder to examine the depth of the scratches she had inflicted upon me.

Together we memorized the dialogues from de Sade's books and recited them to each other, occasionally improvising. She would play the luscious Madame de Saint-Ange and I would be Monsieur Dolmancé. "Tell me, my dear," I asked her, "who intended at your beginnings?"

"My brother," she would answer, taking my bodily jewels into her hands, as if to assess their weight and quality. "The poor darling adored me ever since he was a child, though he never dared to admit it, and he had become the puppet of all the maids in the house. Finally he confessed his desire, and we continued with our intrigue though never all the way. I promised to give myself to him once I was married. . . . Oh, it's so hard! Oh, Pierre, how I love that . . . ! I kept my word. On my wedding night, my husband was so paralyzed by my beauty that he couldn't make love to me, so my brother took command of the situation and finished the task. We indulged in the most divine excesses imaginable, and we even made a pact to mutually serve each other. I procure women for him and he introduces me to the most imaginative, well-endowed men."

"But incest is a crime, isn't it?" I inquired, putting pressure on her thrilling clitoris.

"Well, if we believe that we would have to consider all of Mother Nature's great unions crimes—the very ones she empowers us to perform," she said, fully separating her legs. "Think rationally for a moment: after all the terrible calamities our world has suffered, the human species could hardly have continued to reproduce if it hadn't been for incest. Stop now, Pierre," she whispered, trembling from what was the briefest of orgasms. "Stop for a moment." Muriel took a deep breath. "Do it again, oh, with your fingers," she said, her eyes flashing. "Faster . . . harder . . . Otherwise, the families of men like Adam and Noah would have died out. Do the research, Pierre, study the universal traditions. . . . Oh, wonderful! Go on, please don't stop. . . . All across the world you can find examples of how incest has been tolerated and even considered a most wise and appropriate law for the strengthening of familial ties . . . Very good! That's it! And if love is borne of likeness, who better to cultivate it than brother and sister? Aaaah, Pierre, you are killing me!"

Muriel gave me other books by the very informative Marquis, including *Justine,* which we re-enacted, with her playing Thérèse and me in the role of Clément, one of the monks. We also read *120 Days of Sodom,* which overwhelmed me with the wild gymnastics required to perform various kinds of copulation. To this day I still hold

de Sade in the highest esteem, and I wish erotic literature still gave off that revolutionary crackle of defiance
and contempt. Of course, it has been a long, long time
since his dialogues have had the power to provide me with
relief—the fault, no doubt, being mine and not his.

Once, when I was about seven or eight years old, I
asked my sister to lean against the wall with her arms out-
stretched, as if on a cross. She obeyed, and I must have
felt some kind of special emotion, because as I embraced
her legs I came. My father caught us in that position, and
for various reasons he became furious and scolded me
with uncharacteristic severity, and then slapped me across
the face.

Now it was time for Muriel to make up for what I
had gone through. Lying next to her, I would separate
her round buttocks with one hand and stroke the furrow
between them, moving further and further inside of her
until reaching the soft furry hair at the opening of her
labia. Or I would smother her legs with kisses and licks,
driven to ecstasy by that accumulation of natural delights,
that fragrant skin protecting the little folds of flesh, the
blood vessels and the nerve endings that lay underneath.
I wouldn't have minded dying like that, I thought to
myself, contemplating the curve of her foot at such close
range, or the subtle relief of an ankle bone or a birthmark
on her calf. Sometimes I would concentrate on her feet:
I would put shoes on, take them off, dab her feet with
perfume, paint her toenails, cloak them in transparent silk
handkerchiefs, or place rings on her toes. I would clasp a

jet necklace around her ankle, wrapping it several times around her foot, extending it over the intoxicating arch, and then around her big toe, like a jeweled sandal.

One day she found me admiring my feet, caressing myself. I confessed to her that I pretended they were hers, and then, suddenly, she gave me an unusually demure kiss on the cheek.

One night we stole outside to the garden and climbed up to the top of the oak tree, where we could see into my parents' bedroom. The light was still on, but the balcony window was half-closed and despite our most valiant efforts we could only catch the faintest glimpse of a shirt lying across the back of a chair and the rhythmic movements of two objects which took us some time to identify as two large bare feet fighting against two tiny slippers at the edge of the bed. We watched as one slipper slid down until it dangled from a pair of toes, suspended for what seemed like a long, long time before falling off.

Soon after, I received my first camera already loaded with a roll of film, and I took my first few photographs of Muriel. But since I did not know how to develop film and we could hardly run the risk of allowing some stranger's hands to manipulate her unclothed image, I made her pose in clothing, with lace up to her neck and fanciful hats crowning her head. Our photographic sessions tended to wind down in my bedroom, where she would lie on top of me and rub against my erect penis. She would order me to remain silent, and when it became clear that my restraint was reaching its breaking point, she would stop. I would try to hold back until she came. Then, after a few vigorous waves of pleasure, I would ejaculate onto her belly. Whenever our orgasms coincided or came close to coinciding, it seemed that our bodies were one and the same, and the scar on her chin seemed more mine than hers.

Not long afterward, Muriel fell ill. She grew tired and feverish, and lost her appetite entirely. Her ears and her chest hurt. The doctor's diagnosis was general exhaustion, and he prescribed total bed rest. But my sister had a fire burning inside her, as do so many people who sense death approaching and suddenly become determined to live life in a battle against the clock.

I was in no position to restrain myself either, and the recent change in her appearance hardly displeased me—the opposite, in fact: it worked like an aphrodisiac. She had to stay in bed, but I would visit her in her bedroom as soon as she was alone, and I would lick the curve of her elbows, her breasts, the fiery folds of her inner thighs. Perhaps I too had the sensation that she would be leaving us, and wanted to savor her presence as long as I could, so I could retain a clear recollection of all our crowning moments before the sickness would take her away. It was a miracle that I didn't get infected, too.

One morning she complained of a sharp pain close to her heart. She coughed quite a bit and her breathing was labored. She died around midday, of what was then called the Spanish Influenza. My mother was absolutely devastated and my father sobbed openly, slapping his hands against his head.

That night they agreed to leave me alone with Muriel. She was in her bed. Someone had powdered her scar.

I bolted the door closed. I touched her forehead, still cold with sweat, and I separated the sheets. She was wearing her communion dress, and on her legs she wore a pair of heavy black stockings. Someone once told me—or perhaps I read it somewhere—that there are people who pillage cemeteries and use the mucus-like discharge from snails to lubricate the thighs of the dead bodies in order to have sex with them. At that moment I truly regretted never having entered her. As I caressed her oily thighs, I grew more and more excited and released my juices upon her. The semen slid across her black stockings, creating iridescent little puddles just like the trail left behind in the wake of a snail's path.

Afterward, sitting at her side, I took a photograph of her. It is an image that I have always kept close to me, one which I have copied over and over again in my paintings and which I contemplate as I write these words. In it my body seems to flow from hers, like one of those ectoplasmic emanations that spurious mediums and unscrupulous photographers in the early twentieth century concocted to supposedly reveal the elusive nature of the soul, caught by surprise at the moment of leaving a dead person behind during a seance.

VI

The Great War

When Muriel died—Muriel, who had been my father's closest link to the memory of the beautiful Polish woman—my father felt like he had been widowed all over again. He became more aggressive, more obstinate, more melancholy. He walked through the vineyards talking to himself and waving his hands about, or arguing heatedly with the maître de chai about the sugar level or the acid content of the grape harvest. And while I had hardly ever seen him drink before, I now found myself going down to the wine cellar almost nightly to rescue him from indulging in his libations. Uncorking his most valuable wines at random, scarcely bothering to decant them, he would gaze up at me, his eyes filled with reproach: the Influenza should have taken his son, not his daughter, away from him. I could tell that something had changed in his lovemaking habits, too. From the garden, his bedroom window was often dark now, but I often heard lusty moans—which were in no way moans of grief—escaping from behind his bedroom door. Many times I wondered if those sessions ever brought any pleasure to my mother, for I never once heard the sound of her voice emerge.

I was still too young to feel grief in any real, intense way. I missed Muriel not as a sister but as a companion, a lover, and an irresponsible tutor who had abandoned me in the middle of the school year. In my fantasies I would relive the nights we had shared, and I would invent new pleasures that we had never been able to experience together: I dreamt of ejaculating in her mouth, or of sodomizing her, or of her sucking my nipples and my anus. Together, we would re-create all the endless, hot-blooded orgies we had read about in those ancient volumes. I dreamt of her massaging my erect penis between the soles of her feet, and tickling my purple gland with the tips of her painted toenails until my milky lava bubbled up and gushed forth, sliding down the arch of her foot, warm and tremulous. I had managed to save Muriel's most low-cut shoes and would slide my penis into them until it would emerge from the little opening at the tip like a jubilant, obscene tongue. I rendered my homage to Onan for an entire year in this way.

Hungry for new revelations, I continued to work my way through the library. I read Voltaire's *Philosophical Dictionary,* which fascinated and shocked me, and every last volume of *Jean-Christophe* in the first editions of *Cahiers de la Quinzane,* which my mother had subscribed to and which was no longer being published. As I read Romain Rolland's words I felt my senses grow heightened, coming alive—it was like taking a stroll after a rainstorm, or feeling a gust of ocean wind whip across my face.

I found a copy of Musset's *Gamiani,* with several pages stuck together. It was old enough, I calculated, to have endured the amorous effusions of my great-grandfather. As I carefully separated the pages with a piece of cotton soaked in alcohol, I relived the same glorious sensations that must have inspired my ancestor. To tell the truth, I have always despised continence, and this time was no different. I couldn't resist satisfying myself, and reached my own ecstasy on almost exactly the same passages, though unlike my great-grandfather I took care to turn my member away as I felt myself approaching climax.

There was also an incomplete collection of *Les maîtres de l'amour,* edited by Apollinaire, and a 1907 edition of *Les onze mil verges,* which I found to be quite delightful and whose tone I attempted to imitate many years later when I wrote my own terrible novel, *Le Chevalier d'Eon.*

When the German military robbed Belgium of its sovereignty in August of 1914, my father felt utterly betrayed, and despite my mother's pleas he enlisted immediately in the Armed Forces, delegating the various responsibilities of the vineyards before leaving for the front. We didn't receive word from him for an entire month. I was convinced that he had been killed, but in fact he survived both the Battle of the Marne and the first Champagne offensive. At the end of that December he was granted a furlough, and he came home extremely thin and with a defiant attitude about him, walking around without bending his knees, as if floating on air.

He seemed bewildered by the fact that he still had a family, that he still had the château. I got the feeling he was uncomfortable, and that each night he feared the moment when he would have to go to bed with my mother. As he prepared to return to the front, he shook my hand as if he barely knew me and then smiled broadly as if he had just passed some kind of test.

A few days later, rifling through the drawer where he usually kept the Polish woman's things, I discovered they were missing. I suppose my mother, in a flurry of puritan sentiment, or perhaps jealousy, had thrown them away.

In his last letters, my father wrote to us about the rat-infested trenches and the scavenger birds that circled above the blackened forests of Verdun. But never once did he mention that he had been awarded a military decoration. We found out in March, when we received the official death notification. Unable to speak, my mother simply handed me the communiqué to read. I kissed and hugged her, and for nearly an hour we clung to one another, sobbing.

Afterward I went to the library. Convinced that pleasure was the only thing that could alleviate my pain, I pored through one volume after another of *Les maîtres de l'amour,* searching for those grand moments that would help me reach ecstasy. It was a fruitless effort: all the passages seemed either too childish or too cerebral. The erection I wanted so badly simply refused to materialize on its own, and my persistent manipulation did nothing more than cause a painful congested feeling. My arm was aching, and I was ready to give up hope when, as an afterthought, I opened Restif de la Bretonne's *Anti-Justine,* and read: "She had ejaculated with the third lick of his gifted tongue, and in her delirium she raised her legs high in the air, clicking her heels, elevating her ass to favor the application of her pumper's mouth and the intromission of the tongue with which he was exciting her clitoris. . . . She was the image of her mother in this heel-clicking, for I never rogered that lamented woman save in daytime, for, whether having at her cunt-wardly, bumwise, or orally, I wished to be inspired by the best part of her—I am referring to her leg and foot. I used to ask her to click her heels, because that reminded me of a woman walking—and that would always give me an erection. . . ."

The memory of my sister's bare heels clicking against the inside of her slippers suddenly replaced the mental image this passage had inspired, and I came in a series of violent convulsions that were the precise counterpoint to that clicking. And though I cannot say the experience was altogether pleasurable, it at least afforded me the release I so desperately needed and quelled both my desires and my fears.

I soon discovered several pages stuck together in that copy of the *Anti-Justine,* not with semen but with adhesive tape. They were the pages that contained the anthropophagic episode and the only explanation I can think of is that someone had decided the exploits of the monk Fout-à-Mort—who killed, quartered, and devoured all the women he had sex with—to be slightly excessive.

That night I went to my mother's bedroom, in the hopes of consoling her a bit. I was so tired, however, that I fell asleep in her bed, right by her side. I fell asleep dreaming of a very tall woman whose leg ascended like a column and whose face was obscured from view. Softly she massaged my penis with the tip of a black leather shoe, as soft as kid-gloves, and then tapped at my balls with the tip of her high heel, giving me both pleasure and pain.

I woke up with a healthy erection, and before I knew it, I had lifted up my mother's satin nightgown and penetrated her deeply, all the way through to my sword's haloed hilt. She placed her hands against my shoulders as if to push me away but I held fast to her with an arrogance and force unusual for someone of my age and inexperience, and I rode her insistently, lost in desire as I rocked her back and forth rhythmically.

"Ah, no . . ." she exclaimed weakly. "That's enough, please go now."

But I was too far gone to obey her, and she too had begun to respond to my various attentions. The room was shrouded in inky darkness, and just like in my dream I couldn't quite make out my mother's face. Nevertheless, her arms and legs gripped my body and her lubricated crevice absorbed my thick penis, rubbing it up and down and squeezing it tightly.

"I can't, we've gone too far . . ." she murmured in choked tones. "I can't. This cannot happen."

"Yes, yes," I gasped, pushing into her harder and faster.

I felt as if my mother were sucking me in, as if her salvation depended on my determination. And for an instant I felt my strength beginning to fail me, and I was overcome by panic, but as her soft body began to quiver, my strength and resolve returned. She began to moan, slowly at first then faster and faster, and when she reached orgasm she fell completely silent. Like a diver gulping for air before going underwater, I breathed in her perfume, a mixture of musk and Bulgarian rose, of iris and heliotrope, and with my eyelids pressed shut I let out a voluptuous cry and spilled an abundant tribute inside of her.

Frightened of the brutal reality I would have to face, I didn't dare move. Even my penis resisted, and against all laws of nature it refused to wither away. But when my mother began to cry, I knew I had to stop. As I withdrew from her, my penis made an odd, ironic snapping noise.

She turned her back to me and continued crying, but even her tearful sobs inflamed my youthful appetites. Pressing my belly against her naked ass, I placed my legs between hers. As I kissed the back of her neck, that intoxicating potion of scents intensified. With one hand I caressed her full, robust breasts, trying to span both nipples at the same time. At first I wasn't certain I could reach her pleasure chamber from behind, especially given the awkward position, but in the end I was pleasantly surprised at the flexibility of the maneuver. As she felt my warm, wet head pressing into the lips of her vulva, my mother fell silent once again, like an animal caught by surprise in the middle of the night.

"You're forcing me!" she protested.

But that wasn't true, and her slippery crevice betrayed the magnitude of a desire that she was unable to control.

"Ah, no!" I moaned as she withdrew from me.

"No, no, no!" she repeated, and pushed her ass backward so that I could lunge into her again and impale her fully.

She wavered like that for a long while, like a trout caught on a hook, and I waited for her spasms to slow to a halt before I gently pulled out like a delicate succubus that had visited her in her dreams.

VII

The Death of Sardanapalus

It dawned on me the following afternoon, when my school day ended and I realized I would have to return home that, unlike my antics with Anne-Marie and Muriel, what had occurred between my mother and me could very well change the course of my life. Voltaire, de Sade, and the Christian Brothers' schools—in whose institute I had studied until I was thirteen—had effectively vaccinated me against religion, but they certainly weren't responsible for teaching me to engage in the most prohibited form of incest. With my sister, it was only a game, or at least that's the way I saw it. I hadn't gone very much further with my mother, but with her, somehow, I had nevertheless become a transgressor. My father had just died, and anyone passing judgment upon me would say that I had betrayed his memory.

I hopped on the back of a wagon that was hauling barrels of wine, and I jumped off somewhere near the banks of the Garonne. For hours I wandered through the wall of high poplars and little islands overgrown with reeds. Every so often, with a monotonous regularity— "I'm leaving, I'm leaving"—a boat would glide down the river, and as I admired its resplendent prow piercing through the waters, I imagined it was blasting through a translucent mound of Venus, showering it with a spray of sperm. There were moments when I wondered if the erotic passion of the previous night had just been a figment of my imagination, but the heavy soreness between my legs was the physical memory and evidence of the tremendous pleasure I had enjoyed.

That night I arrived home at the château much later than usual, thirsty and coated with dust. I found my mother already eating her dinner, and I felt her tremble as I deposited a kiss on her cheek. Her face, however, indicated neither anger nor disgust, only anxiety and a faint hint of reproach. The deep circles under her eyes, which should have made her seem ugly, only added a disturbing intensity to her gaze. She wore a black wrap-around dress with a deep décolletage, which seemed especially designed to show off her beauty rather than to satisfy the conventions of mourning.

"I was very worried, Pierre," she said to me. Then, noting my appearance, she sympathetically added, "I can't bear to think of what you have been going through!"

Right then I felt as if she had absolved me of all guilt. After all, what had I really done but expressed my love for her in the most sensually pleasing manner I knew? As I ate my dinner, I stared at her like a feverish animal, unable to banish the thought that the nourishment I needed was her, not the food I was being served. Biting into a pea made me think of her nipples, which at some other time in my life must have been quite familiar to me, and the sight of a curly leaf of kale sprouting up from a bowl made me think of the lushness between her legs. Mentally I undressed my mother, fantasizing about the different parts of her body and how they smelled, how they tasted. I wanted to lick her, suck her, I wanted her to dissolve beneath my tongue, I wanted to fill her completely, please her both as son and lover. My prick grew swollen as I watched her lips curl around and slide down her fork, and I imagined them sliding up and down my penis just as Muriel said they had done to my father's. And as I watched her teeth idly nibbling a rib of lamb, I imagined them sinking into my rod of flesh until she had eaten it away altogether, or else rendered it a shapeless, pulpy mass.

I breathed deeply as I finished my dessert. We were alone now, and she took advantage of the moment to say, in a very somber voice, "What happened between us was beautiful but it was also terrible, especially for me. It would never have happened had I not felt so alone. Please understand that it will never happen again."

She rose up from her chair and left the room, but before disappearing through the door she turned around to look at me. Beyond any maternal concern she may have felt, I couldn't help but note the faintest hint of insouciance in her eyes.

I went to bed, and tried in vain to fall asleep. As I yearned for my mother's skin I was also beset by the recurring thought that we were still under the same roof. I held out my arms in the darkness, kissing the pillow and stroking myself, thinking that I was stroking her and calling out to her and that she, in turn, was responding to me. I did this for a while but finally, I could no longer contain myself and I leaped out of my bed. Clutching the oil lamp, I ran out to the hallway and sped through the labyrinth of corridors until I finally reached her bedroom.

As I stood before her door, I felt my resolve falter. Was I capable of repeating, in an absolutely premeditated manner, something that had happened so spontaneously the night before, practically as we were sleeping? She had voiced her objections and despite all my licentious reading, I suddenly lacked the strength to break my mother's will. Then it occurred to me that there was a marvelously simple method to test the limit of her resolve: the door handle. My heart pounded furiously as I turned it, and then I felt the door give way. But suddenly I was scared again, and I quickly but gently closed the door. There was no doubt about it: she, too, was putting me to the test. I don't know what frightened me more—defying my mother's wishes, or satisfying my own. In either case, I thought, I would surely be punished.

Crouched in the corner of the hallway, next to a tiny potted palm tree, I thought of a passage from *Jean-Christophe* describing the protagonist in the very situation I now found myself in: "His love was so great that he did not dare to indulge in the thing he loved—in fact, the idea frightened him." Now I saw how that sentence, which had seemed weak and prudish before, expressed exactly what I felt. My resolve wavered in time with my eyes, which traveled between the strong light of the oil-lamp and the limpid shadows it cast.

I thought of my mother's legs, of the days when I was a child resting at her feet, unable to conceive of a vision more dazzling than that of her stockings and the iridescent hue they acquired as they hugged the contours of her calves. No sight could be more intoxicating than the motion of my mother's foot as it slid into a pair of shoes, nor was there any sound more suggestive than the clicking of her heels as she walked around her bedroom to pose before her full-length mirror with little ferns etched in its corners. There, she would carefully check to see that no wrinkle, distortion, or stain altered the harmony of her exquisite lower extremities. I would call up the memory of her flirtatious foot, inviting me to play horse with her. And that was when I, prisoner to a powerful erection, ran toward the door of the bedroom where I had been conceived sixteen years earlier.

The door did not budge. My mother had bolted it shut. I tried pushing the door, pounding on it. I would have broken it down if I could have.

"Mother, mother, open the door!" I whispered imploringly.

I heard no response, but I could sense her presence on the other side, close by, holding back her breath, not daring to open the door, not wishing to go to sleep either. Eventually I stopped calling out to her, for fear of rousing the servants, and I remained there on my knees,

desperate with desire and frozen from the cold, until the
dawn light began to creep into the corridor and I realized that the privileges of childhood were no longer
mine. Never again would I suck her breasts nor caress
the smooth flesh of her legs nor revel in the vision of
her feet before my eyes.

The next day, Sunday, there was a mass for my father at the church at Léognan. I didn't want to go, mainly
because the idea of accompanying my mother was torture—being with her would make me feel far worse than
staying home and pining away for her alone. She didn't
come home at lunchtime, and in the evening I excused
myself and ate dinner in my bedroom, claiming I was
indisposed. She didn't come looking for me—perhaps
she was fearful of reopening the wound between us,
or perhaps she smelled a trap, which it might very well
have been.

That was how the bond we shared slowly degener-
ated into a succession of uncomfortable, ill-fated encounters, of impulsive, affectionate gestures that we quickly
curbed, of long silences filled with suspicion. For a while
we tried to pretend we didn't really need each other, and
our easy harmony was torn apart by a steely defiance. We
slowly learned to tolerate each other, and we tried to co-
exist without too much trouble, outside of the concerns
relating to my future. The high-quality Domaine de
Chevalier wines depended upon the staff my father had
assembled, and while I had no desire to dedicate my life
to them, I did not have a clear idea of what I did want to

do, either. Thinking that maybe, like new wines, I needed to breathe a bit, I decided to take a trip. I told my mother I would go to Bordeaux for a week, and two days later I wrote to her from Paris.

Despite the ominous proximity of the front, the cars that had been requisitioned and confiscated, the sand bags piled up at the entrance to Notre-Dame, the multitudes battling each other at the newspaper kiosks along the boulevards to read the war communiqués, the city had not renounced its right to laugh, have sex, and have fun. The women of Paris had picked up where their men had left off, and one couldn't help but thank one's lucky stars for being too young to fight, but old enough to appreciate the sight of so many single women. It was funny, I mused, how the same war that sent my father to his grave had also sent hemlines skyward. Some women, however, like my mother, maintained strict mourning and the Parisians could gauge how the war was going by the number of black veils and dresses floating about the city.

Hungry for adventure, I went everywhere: street after street, cafés to drink grenadine or hot wine, strolls along the tranquil, luminous river, and along the docks where, according to Anne-Marie, my father had found his first wife. As I thought of my mother I realized that our failed relationship had not hardened me—as a result I had become even more emotional, less cynical. In Paris, I found myself accosted by professionals in the art of love, though they were a far cry from my feminine ideal, from that life-sustaining dream of being left utterly breathless and suddenly inspired to cry "Stop!" before the most seductive, thrilling vision I have ever laid eyes on. I suppose I was looking for a woman who resembled my mother, on the outside at least, and without her intransigence.

There were women who came close to my idealized vision, but they were always unattainable. Perhaps it was my lack of courtship experience, or the other man whose arm they clung to, or my lack of means, or all three of those things. I saw one of these women one day in the Tuileries. She wore a very short, pale turquoise dress with matching hat and hung onto the arm of a man who was clearly her lover. She walked in very tiny little steps, as if fearful of losing her balance, and I just stood there, looking at her. She was lovely, with a rosy face and firm breasts. Suddenly, as she turned to face the sun, her body was illuminated by a halo of orange-hued light that shone through her dress and revealed that she wore nothing underneath it. Feeling terribly envious of her lover, I watched them walk away toward some bed where he would soothe the arousal caused by the light chafing of silk against her tender skin.

Later, at the Louvre, when I entered the room with *The Death of Sardanapalus,* the tumultuous sensuality inside of me finally erupted. Standing before that tableau of jumbled bodies, larger than life, that masterwork of color and dramatic tension, my penis grew hard and began to pulsate beneath my pants. I didn't know what I admired more: the indolence of Sardanapalus, who from

the heights of his bed attends to the voluntary immola-
tion of all those who have brought him pleasure; the
marvelously endless shoulders and back of the Circassian
slave who hugs the bed where she has enjoyed so many
lascivious delights; the determination of the Bactrian
woman in the background who hangs from one of the
columns holding up the roof to save herself from perish-
ing at the hands of a slave; or the golden- and rose-hued
silhouette of another slave, whose body is gripped by
something that could be ecstasy the very moment she is
stabbed. My eyes traveled down the figure of this slave
woman, lingering on her pearl earrings, the bold contours
of her throat, the double curve of her breasts, the endless
profile of her hips, and the concave dimple of her lower
back flowing into her monumental ass, down her robust,
sinuous legs, until reaching that delectable foot, bound
up in a thick bracelet and covered with a diaphanous
golden slipper that just barely covered her toes, curled
backward to reveal almost the entire sole, in her final
spasm of life.

My attentions were focused on that one area, a little
hole which seemed like Delacroix's allusion—either con-
scious or not—to the vaginal crevice, delineated by the
taut arch surrounded by folds of white material. I was
tempted to move away, but I already felt the tickle, the
bubbling juices, and the stiffness in the belly that precede
orgasm. My trapped penis leaped with a vengeance, and
for the first and only time in my life I ejaculated without

touching or rubbing myself at all. An unusually explosive spasm of pleasure shook through my body as I clenched my teeth to keep from screaming.

There were very few people in the room, but one man approached me. Solicitously, he asked me if I needed anything.

"No, thank you," I replied. "I'm just a bit overwhelmed."

He quickly informed me that Stendhal had often suffered dizzy spells and occasionally had fainted before some or other work of art, and then went on to explain that this was very common among people with heightened sensibilities. Then he noticed the stain that had begun to appear on my pants and, somewhat perplexed, he added: "But well, I've never seen it quite to that degree . . ."

I left the Louvre feeling somewhat ashamed of myself, but duly convinced that I wanted to be a painter. There was no doubt about it: a profession that gave such great pleasure had to be a good thing.

VIII

The Camel's Mare

During that first period in Paris, I made an effort to meet cold, aloof women, who generally considered me either too young or too inept: rather than an attempt to fulfill my desires, I took it as a personal challenge. There was the Belgian émigré who lived in the same hotel as I did, who never answered the questions I asked and who seemed to look straight through me as if I didn't exist; or the salesgirl in the flower shop who grudgingly agreed to see me on three successive dates and never showed up for a single one; or the girl who walked alone through Monceau Park and who resisted my tenacious overtures by clubbing me with her parasol.

Even now, at this stage in my life, only a few hours from the end, I never cease to be amazed at my inadequacy in the art of seduction. How very little I learned from the characters of Choderlos de Laclos and de Sade. It isn't for lack of trying and after all, I do have some proof of my more successful efforts: Tutune, for example, and my wife, and Marayat, to a certain degree. But the truth is, I have always preferred to be conquered than to be the conqueror myself. Anne-Marie and Muriel had been so

57

easily accessible that I had grown accustomed to having my desires satisfied rather effortlessly. And thinking about it now, I believe those desires were so evident that when I attempted to disguise them, I simply seemed insincere. It didn't take long for me to discover that it was far easier, both physically and emotionally, to frequent one brothel over and over again or to search for this ideal woman inside of me, than to actually go out and try to find that woman myself, for I would only fall in love with her and risk losing her. I have done the exact opposite of what most men do: I have appropriated and adopted the most seductive qualities of all the women I have known, and in my own way I have been able to desire all women in myself. But I no longer feel that attraction I once felt for my own image—enveloped in lace, touched up and molded into my own mythical vision of myself. What will the anatomy students think as they prepare to open my corpse and discover my painted toenails?

Frightened by the sex professionals constantly accosting me in the streets, but hungrier than ever to take home something more substantial than a few stolen moments in front of *The Death of Sardanapalus,* I made a few inquiries and was recommended to Chez Suzanne on the Rue Monsieur le Prince near the Boulevard St. Germain. From the outside it looked like a slightly out-of-date clothing shop, with a window display lined with mirrors blocking the view inside. In front of the mirrors was a lineup of dismembered female mannequins, busts of faces, necklines, and hands. The busts were made of papier-mâché, fleshed out with cotton padding and decorated with some loose swaths of fabric, though the hair on their heads looked convincingly real. They wore no clothes.

A little bell rang and I entered an empty room illuminated only by tiny wall sconces. A thirtyish woman, her hair piled on top of her head, dressed in black, with thick, matronly arms, attended my arrival. She had an attractive, dynamic face that seemed to suggest a spark of good humor as well.

"Good afternoon," she said. "May I help you? I am Madame Ulianov."

"I'm not sure," I replied. Suddenly I was afraid that I had been the victim of some kind of misunderstanding or a practical joke. Little did I know then that I would soon become a whorehouse habitué.

Madame Ulianov looked me up and down.

"Does it have something to do with love?" she asked, with an encouraging smile.

I nodded. She asked my age.

"Eighteen," I lied.

"And how did you get out of the war?"

I told her that I had been exempted for health reasons.

"I do hope," she said playfully, "that it isn't contagious."

She guided me into a larger, better-lit room filled with ottomans and little side tables, where four young women, each one different from the others, sat dressed in nothing but their high heels. As they saw me enter, they gathered in a circle around me and smiled invitingly, hands on hips.

"They're all free. You can choose the one who most pleases you," said Madame Ulianov.

I was stunned by the display of female nudity. Although they seemed to have been selected more for the overall group effect than for their individual qualities, they were certainly all young and ripe. I couldn't resist glancing down at their shoes—a very varied display—and Madame Ulianov took note of this immediately.

"Ah! I see our friend has his penchants. What would you prefer, sir? Satin slippers with swan feathers, ankle boots, above-the-knee boots, pumps?" she asked me as she pointed to each girl's shoes.

"I can't decide. They're . . . they're all so lovely," I stammered, but my compass had already begun to point in the direction to which it was attracted. I stretched my hand out to a girl barely a few years older than I was. She wore satin slippers, and the sight of her bare arch decorated by a white feather took my breath away.

Véronique had small breasts, wide hips, and a faint hint of dark fur between her pale thighs. First I paid Madame Ulianov, then we walked toward a door upholstered in a worn-out, vermilion-colored leather, which opened onto a hallway with rooms on either side. The girl opened one of the doors, walked in, lay down on the bed, and waited for me to remove my clothes. Through the paper-thin walls, we could hear wanton gasps and agonizing howls.

Something—the unfamiliar surroundings, the cold atmosphere—had caused my erection to wane, but my able companion lay me down on my back and began to attend to my faltering member. She sucked it, tugged a bit, and then, like a potter molding clay, began to massage it gently until it regained more respectable dimensions. She wet her fingers and then slipped them into her lips, half-hidden by her downy fur, to lubricate her luscious tunnel. Then she straddled my belly and I felt her guide my penis into her warm shelter.

"There we go!" she exclaimed with delight as she came down hard on my thighs and began to ride me.

This time my insecurity did not get the best of me, and I began to respond to her movements. Her breasts, moving rhythmically back and forth, and her thighs, roughly pumping me up and down, drove me wild. Her body slammed against my stomach in crashing jolts, coming faster and faster before stopping short suddenly. My tenacious amazon stopped for a moment and took a few deep breaths before resuming, faster and faster until reaching a breakneck pace. Véronique threw her head back, as if offering up her neck to me. Suddenly I thought of the lovely Polish woman, galloping toward the ocean, and I felt the urge to stroke the hair that whipped against the amazon's shoulders. But I didn't. My hands simply scratched through the air as I spilled out with a loud moan and she prolonged my ecstasy with a few more rounds of the same. Immediately afterward, while her warm nest still cradled my shuddering member, through the wall I heard another man shout "Ahh . . . ahh" in crescendo and I felt my own orgasm reach out and fuse into his.

"Did I do it too fast?" the young woman asked me as she dismounted me, afraid she sensed disappointment.

I admitted that the end had come earlier than I had expected, and she offered to do it again, but I only had enough money for the hotel and my return ticket back to the château.

"If I could, I would do it for free," Véronique said. "But Madame is very strict about that. But please, do come back when you're in Paris again. The next time will be much better."

The following morning, after closing my door on my way out, I spied a pair of women's shoes, freshly cleaned, in the hallway next to one of the doors. They were high heels, black, with a strap that crossed the top of her foot diagonally until meeting another strap with a buckle at the ankle. As I walked down the stairs, I furtively hid the shoes in my travel bag.

Before boarding the train, I went to see the female camel in the Jardin des Plantes. She was the talk of Paris: she had been found wandering through the countryside near the front, and at first the French authorities assumed that she had come with one of the Senegalese or Algerian battalions, so they took her to the zoo where the state would provide her with food and shelter like a heroine of the trenches.

That had been a few months earlier. Later they discovered that she had actually been part of a circus, and that she had never had to face von Kluck's soldiers. In light of this, her many admirers lost interest in her, with the exception of one stout little family man who scaled the thick walls of the Jardin des Plantes one night, entered the property, and was then caught by surprise in the middle of a most amorous moment with the camel.

The newspapers reported that the guard on duty held back a bit before apprehending them, not wanting to intrude on such a tender encounter. In the cafés where people were usually embroiled in heated arguments about some or other battle at the front, and accusing some general of playing dirty politics, they now speculated as to whether this was a case of rape or if, in fact, the lady camel had given her consent to the little man.

As I mentioned, I went to pay her a visit. She had a saucy little hump with a crown of hair like a tonsured priest, and long, curly eyelashes. Chewing on a few blades of straw, she ambled over to me from a primitive hut where she had her shelter and bed. Parading before me like a model down a runway, she proudly showed off her leonine flanks and then retreated. There was something seductive in those undulating movements but, in the end, she wasn't really my type.

There were very few other passengers on my train, and at Poitiers my car emptied out. Suddenly, I found myself gripped by a desperate urge, probably due to the sun shining directly down between my legs. At first I thought to relieve myself with my hands, but man is an instinctively inventive creature, and tends toward creativity whenever the opportunity arises. Fortunately, I was not unprepared. From my traveling bag I removed one of the woman's shoes that I had pilfered from the hotel, and caressed it as I placed it upon my fleshy protuberance. I began to tug at them, one inside the other and both at the mercy of the train's rumble, until I could no longer contain myself and I spilled my effusions beneath the sun, in seven splendid paroxysms, a perfectly calibrated dose of voluptuous afternoon libations.

IX

The Oleander Poison

My mother scolded me for having gone to Paris without her consent, but forgave me when I told her how the trip had helped me find my vocation. Together we decided that I would register at the École des Beaux-Arts at Bordeaux.

One afternoon, on my way back home after a walk through l'Eau Blanche, I was struck by some kind of omen. Something was about to happen. I surveyed the landscape before me and from a distance I thought I could see the evanescent image of the Polish woman looking out a window in one of the château's towers. Although she hadn't made an appearance in three or four years, I was certain it was her, because nobody ever went up to those towers. Surrendering to my childish impulses I broke into a run. On the outdoor patio, bare-chested men lifted heavy crates of grapes.

As I reached the first-floor landing, I heard footsteps descending the staircase. Frightened that my heavy breathing would give me away, I took a few steps backward and ducked in the library. From behind the partially open door I could hear my mother walking downstairs, and the maître de chai following her from a certain distance away. Overwhelmed by shock and suspicion, I groped for something—anything—to cling to and grabbed the first book I saw. I tried to read, but the words danced before my eyes as if sliding across a drum.

When we reconvened for our afternoon snack, I found myself contemplating the same serene beauty as always, but today there was a note of satisfaction on her face, of a consummated desire, that could hardly be attributed to the flavor of the madeleines and the café crème. Her eyes were radiant, and her natural fragrance seemed more pungent than usual. My hands still tremble when I think of it. As usual we flipped through the newspapers; for the past few days they had been filled with reports on the Franco-British offensive at Artois. But neither of us was really reading. Her comments were distracted, and it was obvious that she wasn't paying much attention to me. I imagine her thoughts kept wandering back to whatever had been going on in the tower.

Shortly afterward she excused herself and went upstairs to her bedroom. The tower door was locked shut, and there was no way I could force it open without raising eyebrows, but in my father's desk I found a key that fit perfectly in the lock. As I turned it I heard a deep sigh and I got scared, thinking that either somebody was in there or I was about to come face to face with the ghost. Finally I entered. The room was in complete disarray, littered with paintings, furniture, trunks, and other dusty objects. I heard the sigh again. A gray pigeon suddenly stopped its cooing, spread its wings, and flew out the open window.

At the foot of the window, I noticed that a pair of thin hands had left their mark in the dust on the unusually wide ledge. With the determination of an inquisitor, I hunted for the evidence I needed. I couldn't separate what I had seen from what I thought I had seen, and I still don't know to what point I was able to fully grasp what had happened.

Alongside an old trunk, I noticed a series of footsteps in the dust, and it appeared that someone had sat down on the trunk's lid. A lumpy, moth-eaten bed lay on the floor and a crumpled curtain had been tossed onto the floor next to it after having been used to wipe the dust off a table. My conclusion: the ritual had commenced on foot, but the trunk lid had been too uncomfortable, the attempt on the bed had failed, and the sacrifice had finally been consummated on the table. My hypothesis was confirmed by a bit of dried mud on the floor next to the table, which no doubt had sprung loose from the maître's shoes during their struggle.

I could have retched right then and there. I felt snubbed and humiliated, my virility and trust wounded. Most people love making light of adolescent passions, but the power those passions wield is undeniable, as they guide you through those tumultuous years until eventually you must tame them in order to enter the world of adulthood. What child has never felt the desire to kill his parents, or envisioned them kneeling before him to be sacrificed, begging for forgiveness for all their injustices? I, for one, have never lost the capacity to feel things so intensely, and this is what has led me so far from the rules of etiquette and conventions, of the classic concepts of decorum and social status. Almost effortlessly, I can still return and relive the fervor of those days, that anguish that made my stomach churn and my bile rise.

The idea that my mother would give herself to a stranger instead of to me was more than I could bear. I knew I had to go away somewhere—far away, so that I could forget it all. But before I did so I needed to take my revenge. Had that been their first time together? Would I kill both of them, or just her?

Once, when I was a child, I had peeked into that trunk and found a ship captain's uniform, swords, and flintlock muskets that belonged to an ancestor of mine who had fought in the battle of Trafalgar before wandering off to an unknown land somewhere between the Antilles and Mexico. I picked through those remains: the pock-marked, moth-eaten uniforms, the rusty, warped pistol barrels with the flint hooks either missing or damaged. I entertained myself by tossing the curtain up into the air and slicing through it with a saber—the kind that pirates used for commandeering ships and the best-preserved weapon of the lot, though the least appropriate of that expired arsenal. Later, when I had calmed down a bit, I remembered how the maître de chai had once rescued me when I had gotten trapped in a wine press, and

I decided that my mother must have been the one to lead him to the tower and stage the seduction.

Somewhere I had heard about the toxic properties of oleander, but I had never had the occasion or reason to prove it. Now I pulled some leaves off a branch, crushed them into little pieces, ground them up, and mixed them with water. With the precision of a madman I pilfered a meatball from the dinner table, soaked it in the solution, and fed it to one of our cats, which I had locked in the library to make sure it couldn't escape from my clutches.

The cat slowly nibbled at the meatball as if not fully convinced by its flavor, but she eventually finished it off. Half an hour later her body began to tremble and shake. First she scratched frantically at the furniture, then she tried to scale the bookshelves, and finally she crawled toward the door, all the while meowing for help. Her pupils were dilated now, and she looked at me in anguish. I stopped watching her for a little while and not long afterward I found her lying in a corner with wide-open, motionless eyes, her mouth foaming. She wasn't dead, not yet. As I stared at her, her sphincter relaxed and she expelled a yellowish, nauseating liquid of some sort.

There was still one problem left to work out: how to introduce the poison into a madeleine. I solved the problem with a syringe. I didn't dare raise the dosage. I let a few days go by so that nobody would connect the two deaths, and one afternoon when I arrived in the salon a few minutes before my mother, I injected the lethal liquid into a madeleine. I wrapped the syringe in a handkerchief and hid it in my pocket. Then I opened the newspaper and pretended to concentrate on the Central Empire's conquest of Poland.

When my mother arrived, the café crème was served. I had turned the plate around in such a way that the madeleine in question sat as close to her as possible, but there were five others and I had no way of knowing if she would pick the poisoned one. She picked a safe one first, and I followed suit. We sat there, chewing in unison.

"Is something the matter?" she asked me, intrigued by my solicitous behavior.

I shook my head no, and she returned to her reading. Then, as if struck by a premonition, she made a comment about how the Germans had started using chlorine gas in the trenches. And then she lifted the poisonous madeleine off the plate without looking at it, and just as she was preparing to bite into it, I shouted, "No!," throwing myself against her and slapping it out of her hand. The madeleine hit the wall and fell to the floor. Terrified, my mother ran for cover behind her chair and looked at me as if I were a complete stranger.

"I was going to poison you," I said as she returned to her chair. "Forgive me. You know how I want you, you know how I feel about you."

I confessed that I had seen her come down from the tower with her lover. She neither confirmed nor denied anything. I began to cry and she came over to me, stroking my hair as I looked down at her legs and my irrepressible member began to fantasize again on its own. My mother must have noticed, because she jerked back and told me that it would be best if I left immediately, seeing as how we had already decided I would go to the art school in Bordeaux. She insisted that the château would always be my home, but that she would prefer if I didn't return.

The next day we said good-bye. I felt weightless as we kissed one last time. My mother wanted to make sure that I did not lack for anything and asked me how much money I would need. I told her that I would be happy with what the angels lived on—it was a reference to the vineyard: they say that approximately five percent of the wine in the barrels evaporates through the wood, and that was what I said I'd live on. She took this literally and said she would issue me an annual allowance amounting to five percent of the profits from each season's vintage.

X

The Flaming Vulva

It doesn't seem possible that the love you feel for a woman might be arbitrary, but consider this: if you lived on one street and not another, in one city and not another, or by walking into one whorehouse and not the one next door, the crucial moments of your erotic life would be radically different.

Although I had a guaranteed source of subsistence, I was in no condition to be throwing my money around. Luckily I found a tiny apartment on the Place de la Bourse, number 12, an attic flat with two rooms and a kitchen. The view of the river and its location in one of the most beautiful architectural enclaves in France, however, compensated for its miniscule dimensions. Some nights, when I would walk through the deserted city, the facades of the buildings in Bordeaux seemed like something out of a dream, and I fantasized that I was one of the few people who actually lived in those ghostly homes I walked past.

The École des Beaux-Arts was housed inside an old Benedictine abbey, complete with cloister, which not long before had served as a hospice for the infirm. The professors, award-laden "masters" of their profession, had only just begun to digest impressionism—almost a half-century late. Some of them would reluctantly admit that Cézanne, who had died ten years earlier, was a great painter, but they were all adamantly opposed to the Cubists and they abhorred the Fauves. Although I disagreed with their notions, I did want to develop my technique, and I paid close attention to them as they initiated me in the crafts of perspective, *trompe-l'oeil,* and color.

Drawing plaster reliefs bored me, but I did enjoy painting landscapes and real-life nudes. Occasionally the models would pose for us, their thighs wide open, as if waiting for a lover. Their fleshy vulvas would dilate and open wide whenever they felt our eyes converge upon them, or when a ray of sun would bathe them in light, revealing their luscious wetness. Their faces, however, were not always as lovely as their bodies. Socializing with them was complicated, because when class ended their boyfriends would be waiting for them, lurking around the cloister like monks in heat. If one of them was late, a girlfriend would stand guard as we all hovered watchfully behind columns, a bevy of art students stroking our pricks beneath our trousers, waiting for opportunity to strike, which it never did.

Often, instead of climbing the high staircase that led to my apartment, I would go to the brothel or stroll around the fountain of the Three Graces, which rose up in the middle of the Place de la Bourse. In a kind of prelude to the passion I would later develop for dolls and mannequins, I would gaze longingly at the seductive bronze statues and the water cascading down the tight folds of their tunics. Later, back in my attic, I would allow myself to revel in the sensations those moments would inspire. Like a witch doctor scattering a pile of bones on the ground in an attempt to read the future, I would place a bit of lingerie or one of Muriel's or my mother's shoes before me, along with the photographs I had taken of my dead sister or ones I had clipped from a saucy magazine, and I would offer up my jubilant homage to them. Just like my father, I had begun to assemble my own little collection of erotic objects, and I played out this scene so many times that whenever it was hot outside, the entire attic would reek of the sweet smell of semen.

One night, after feeling an unusually urgent lust for the model of the moment, it occurred to me that the most natural way to manifest my adoration would be to masturbate before her image—that is, an image I had created of her. I placed my sketch against the back of a chair and gently shook my eager, impatient penis, like someone shaking a cup of dice. I felt the sap rising, the imperious rumble, and then the final burst, which I spilled forth directly onto the canvas. As the semen slid across the paper I noticed how the colors acquired a brilliant sheen and it occurred to me that semen might add a lovely luster to my paintings and make them more elastic, just like the egg yolks the old masters used. Further tests confirmed my theory. Ever since then I have always mixed my oils with semen. I keep a transparent jar in the refrigerator and fill it according to my artistic needs. Those utilitarian masturbations, however, are often somewhat less pleasurable, because they require the use of a condom. I can scarcely imagine the troubled expressions on the policemen's faces when they search my apartment and discover the jar with my latest emissions.

The first painting to which I applied this technique was a portrait of Muriel in green and yellow tones, based on the photograph I had taken next to her coffin. In my painting, my body seems to emerge, rather shyly, from one of her ribs, between her flattened breasts, like a heretical vision of the myth of Adam and Eve. That photograph served as the inspiration for several different paintings, but the first version is the only one I still have. Despite the passage of time, it still sparkles like a jewel thanks to the generous quantity of semen I used.

Toujours pret: that could have been my insignia. I had plenty of sexual potency to squander back then, to the point that I even slept with women I didn't particularly care for. But there is something called love of the object—female flesh—that is also profoundly sexual and is far different from all conventional notions of beauty. I have surprised myself at times by kissing an opulent belly or a pair of sagging breasts or a leg covered with varicose veins, all in the name of carnal love. I was so excitable that the most casual glance at a dress with a deep neckline or a pair of calves walking down the street would haunt me relentlessly until I could find a way to relieve myself. All that has changed now. The desire remains, but the pleasure takes so much more time. I have lost the notion of urgency. And what good is a desire that cannot be satisfied in the exact moment it strikes?

Madame Ravel's was the most welcoming brothel—the one where I found the friendliest service—and it was in the neighborhood where I lived. In addition to the main salon, there was a restaurant on the ground floor, and the bedrooms were up on the second floor. Many of her clients moved effortlessly from one necessity to the other, from food to sex, and the most frequent habitués looked upon fornication as a complement to the other activities there, as if it were dessert. After the post-dinner drink, a hush would fall over the crowd, as people let their arguments idle so they might express themselves more freely with their bodies.

I fell for Tutune the first time I laid eyes on her in the salon. She must have been relatively new to the house. She was slender and taller than I was, and even though a bit of money was all that was necessary to gain her attentions, she seemed so elusive. She had skin the color of coal, big eyes and dark, protruding lips that turned outward like those of a fish. She laughed easily, and spoke in a singsong voice, constantly altering its pitch, something that took me a while to get used to. And while other people might regard that kind of disposition as a sign of foolishness, in her it seemed to reveal a generosity of spirit. I felt good hearing her laugh—it was like a precious little gift. As I watched her, the man she was sharing a cocktail with made up his mind, and together they went upstairs.

That night I had to resign myself to one of her companions, but it was Tutune I thought of as I began my vigorous ascent to pleasure.

I was luckier the second time around. She approached me the minute I came into the salon, walking in a long stride that gave her an odd kind of elegance, and coyly she asked me if I wanted something to drink. Summoning up my strength and lifting my gaze skyward, I told her that I always grew thirsty after, not before.

She wore a jade-green slip and stockings that matched the color of her skin. A bit later as I looked at her in bed, naked and black against the white sheets, with that little fleshy, pink, hairless crevice, a gasp of surprise escaped from my lips and from that very instant I felt the tug of an emotional bond connecting me to her. It was more than intense physical attraction; it was a magical vision, the wild love of an orientalist painter, the sudden urge to take a palette filled with different colors and stretch the canvas along the floor and let the paint fall in little rivulets onto its surface.

I laid down next to her and stared for a long while at those tempting lips between her legs, so open, so tender, so vulnerable to the eye, making such a spectacular contrast against the rest of her skin, like a flame rising up from a volcano's lava. Somehow, Tutune seemed more naked than any other woman I had ever seen before.

"Is this the latest style?" I asked her.

"No, it's an old Senegalese custom. It's very comfortable, and much more hygienic. Don't you like it?"

The folds of flesh were surprisingly soft and warm to the touch.

"Can't you tell?" I said, pointing to my penis, which trembled impatiently.

If her vulva was warm on the outside, the inside burned like an oven. I almost had to withdraw—the feeling was like dipping your foot in a bath of scalding water—but instead I buried myself in her depths with a forceful thrust, hardly the gentle touch to which she was accustomed. Suddenly, her vagina began pulsating with life.

I became her prisoner without doing a thing: just gazing at her mouth, at those lips that seemed outlined in black, at her breasts with their protruding little nipples. Tutune barely moved at all on the outside, but she drew me in farther and farther, deeper and deeper until I reached the liberation of orgasm. She continued to squeeze the juice from me for a long while, and for a moment, just when I was about to pull out, I thought I was going to remain trapped inside her, unable to withdraw. Finally, my penis made a noise, like the sound of a bottle being uncorked, and Tutune began to laugh again and said that was a sign of good luck.

I couldn't resist one more admiring glance at that incandescent cunt that operated like an independent organism, and for which the battle of legs and asses was absolutely irrelevant in the quest for pleasure. I asked her if she shaved it every day.

"I don't shave it," she said. "I pluck it."

"One hair at a time?"

"Well, yes, obviously."

As I gazed at Tutune, her hairless cave began to tremble again and my offering slowly trickled out from her. At that point, I half expected a curl of smoke to emerge, as well. I placed my head between her open thighs and kissed her luscious lips.

"What are you doing?" said Tutune, interrupting me as her fingers twisted through my hair.

"I want to give you pleasure."

"No, not here. No," she said. "I don't like to mix work with pleasure. I'd be dead in a week! If you want, you can have me again."

I rested alongside her as she massaged my soft penis and made it grow. The contrast between the perfect control of her internal muscles and the relative clumsiness of her hand could not have been more disconcerting, but that naked vulva had cast a spell on me, and the incentive of possibly penetrating it again quickly revived me.

This time the entry was much smoother. I slid into her insides as if on ice skates, and the freshness of my remaining semen cooled her burning heat.

XI

The Women of Ebony

I t was possible that I would be called into service if the war continued. In those days, I often took trips to the countryside in search of landscape ideas, but now, given that I was not interested in getting killed in a trench, I used the excursions to familiarize myself with the use of arms. I bought an old Mauser (which proved too heavy to carry along with my painting equipment) and a six-bullet revolver that now sits on the bedside table next to the bed where I do my writing. Since I am not a hunter by nature, I satisfied myself by aiming at the treetops.

I have always felt that target practice and physical love have a way of clearing the mind and sharpening the vision, and as such are excellent exercises for cultivating the painter's craft. When I was younger I was only able to paint if I had had sex or masturbated beforehand, and perhaps my excessive virility was what prevented me from being able to concentrate. In any event, the last time I made love was weeks ago when Sieglinde left, and lately I have been working more on my photographic montages than on my paintings. And as far as target shooting . . . no, I refuse to succumb to that facile, negative hopelessness.

Around that time there were several group exhibitions that one could participate in without having to leave Bordeaux: the Salon of the Society of Friends of the Arts, the Salon of Decorative Arts, the École de Beaux-Arts' end-of-the-year exhibition of student projects, the annual show of the Applied Arts department of the Gironde, the Salon des Dessignateurs, the Salon d'Automne. . . . Even so, it was little more than an empty spectacle put on by the intellectually responsible society types who only pretended to be interested in the plastic arts. They generally favored the works they considered tasteful and rebuffed the more avant-garde pieces. Given the situation, it was hardly surprising that all the talented and most innovative Bordeaux painters had left the city: Odilon Redon and Albert Marquet at the end of the century, and Andre Lhote around 1910.

I have raised my pencil to write—I always write with a pencil, just to be different—and suddenly I am struck by the vision of an alternative life in a different world. I see myself in the château, knocking on the door to my mother's bedroom, and this time the door opens. I see myself in Paris in 1956, at the exhibition of my paintings, the one that Breton organized, only now I receive warm accolades from my fellow surrealists as well as art critics and buyers, all of whom fight over my canvases. I buy an apartment with windows overlooking the Seine, move in and spend my days making love to voluptuous film stars, naked beneath their wet slickers.

If I have barely ever left Bordeaux, it is only because of laziness, stubbornness, and this notion I have that in my line of work my place of residence matters very little— in this age of rapid communication my merits would be recognized no matter where I happened to live, wouldn't they? Here, at the very least, I have been able to escape all outside influences, and find my own way in the world.

I sold my first painting in the École des Beaux-Arts' end-of-the-year exhibition: a rather conventional depiction of the Port de la Lune, that extended curve created by the Bordeaux docks. I envisioned myself quite the celebrated painter, toasted by the multitudes, pursued by women. To celebrate I went to Madame Ravel's, ordered two bottles of champagne, and locked myself in a room with Tutune.

I wanted to fill my eyes and all my senses with her, and I began to kiss her from the steely tips of her nipples to her elongated, oddly idyllic toes that seemed to have walked out of a classical painting. As for everything in between those two points, I didn't want to miss one single curve, dimple, protuberance, fold, or furrow, but Tutune was pure African austerity and anything that deviated from the conventional intimate embrace made her uncomfortable. She was fidgety and uneasy, and urged me to enter her.

"Well if I have no other choice . . ." I said, my voice hoarse with desire.

I entered her fiery hot oven with the necessary precaution, and she encouraged me by separating her legs as far as she could, vigorously stroking my naked back. Then her internal muscles became a vise and gripped my tool like a hand. She stroked my ass, lightly scratching it. She opened her mouth a bit and ran her tongue across her lips, looking straight at me all the while as she continued milking me. I desperately hoped that those little details were signs of her incipient feelings for me, that they were more than just professional dexterity. I let out a long, luxuriant sigh as I poured my liquor into her open dunes.

"You're tired," she said, relaxing her grip.

"No, no," I responded. "I'm just saving myself for more."

We opened the first bottle, drank from it, and I began kissing her again, nibbling at her and stroking her with my tongue. I wanted to bring her to a quiver, I wanted to discover the key that would unlock her hidden orgasm. I was intrigued that she was so passive, despite her skilled intimacy. As I delicately licked the arch of her ebony foot my prick grew hard again, and I separated her legs so that I might sink into her hairless lips.

"Do you always do it twice?" she asked me shortly afterward, after the fireworks had ended.

"This," I bragged, pouring a few drops of champagne onto her coffee-bean navel, "is only the beginning."

She began to laugh, peals of that contagious laughter, as I resumed my attack. I kissed her eyelids, sucked her earlobes, breathed in the scent of her underarms, sipped the contents of her navel, rubbed against her ass and thighs. I lavished her with all the caresses I had learned and even tried to recall ones that I had never employed, those that I had read about in the château library. But my third effort to arouse her only resulted in my own arousal yet again. Although slightly reluctant, my choked member came back to life and injected her with a smaller but especially gratifying dose, perhaps because it was achieved with greater effort.

Tutune did not want to drink any more, but I opened the second bottle anyway. When Madame Ravel knocked at the door, I told her not to worry, that I would pay for the entire night. My erotic efforts, however, were challenged by all the alcohol I had consumed and I soon fell asleep. Every so often I would awaken to see Tutune's jet-black figure lying next to me, just as she was after the last time I penetrated her: her neck resting against the pillow, her arms at her sides, and her legs slightly open. Her sharp breasts rose and fell to the slow rhythm of her breathing. Only once, around four or five in the morning, did I feel strong enough to resume action. My penis was so sensitive by that point, and I don't know where I found the energy to continue, but I adjusted my body to hers and began to move. She didn't respond; she seemed like an age-old totem pole in the depths of the jungle, destroyed by a thunderstorm. The situation reminded me of a story—by Mac Orlan, I think—about a fisherman who returns home in the middle of the night, very tired, and makes love to his wife in the dark, not realizing that she is dead.

When dawn broke I asked Tutune to come with me to my attic. She said no, but seemed touched by all the time and effort I devoted to her. Somehow I got her to agree, though reluctantly, to visit me as soon as she had a day off.

Even to masturbate I had to summon her image. I only realized the extent of my dependence one afternoon, when our date was postponed yet again. I went to the brothel and found her busy with someone else. Aroused by the temptation of infidelity, I decided to take another girl that night. But my prick failed in the middle of the act, and it was only resuscitated after much patience, vivid imagination, and repeated licking.

Finally, when the hour of our date arrived, I went to pick her up. I stood there marveling at how she looked, for until then I had only seen her either nude or in lingerie. She wore a dress with a deep décolletage, her breasts peeping out like little bits of quince. Despite the motley mixture of colors—ivory, orange, pink, pea green—her look was like that of the ladies of the First Empire. As we walked down the street I could hear the murmur of the passersby, who stepped out of our way to look at her.

I already had a vigorous erection as we climbed my stairs and I followed her, admiring her tight ass beneath her dress. Once we got into my apartment she scrutinized everything inside. First she looked at my paintings and then she looked back at me, as if surprised that I was actually their author.

To encourage her sexual metamorphosis, I installed a mirror in the bedroom. We took off our clothes and now, no longer hindered by the obstacle of location, I asked her to surrender herself to me. I explored her warmth with my fingers for a long time, and finally her breathing grew heavier and heavier, and at last I began to notice an incipient wetness. Over and over I would bring her to the edge of climax and then pause. She moaned, arching her body backward; both our backs were bathed in perspiration. When I decided she had had enough, I directed my tongue into her clitoris, stimulating it as my fingers fluttered away, incandescent.

Suddenly she exhaled in one long, final gasp and her body shook—rather weakly, I thought, for a woman of her size and stature. But then, just when I had assumed it was all over, a series of very light vibrations began to take over her body, growing and growing until she exploded in one final burst of energy and all the muscles in her body contracted. As she trembled in orgasm, her slender legs grew hard as steel, and her feet tightened up and bucked back. Balancing on her bottom, she shook her arms as if swimming backstroke until they found the bedposts behind her. Finally I understood what she meant that day in the brothel when she told me she would be dead within a week if she gave in to pleasure all the time.

For a long time she lay there exhausted. Then, laughing, she pointed out a nail that had broken during her battle with the bedposts. When I asked her if she wanted to come and live with me, her face grew very somber and she turned her back to me. Looking at herself in the mirror she said yes, as long as Madame Ravel approved.

Madame complained a bit. Apparently, the wild contrast between Tutune's submissive exterior and her volcanic vagina had attracted a fair share of admirers, and Madame Ravel accused me of stealing one of her best students. She then made me promise that I wasn't luring Tutune away to exploit her, and yet she refused to accept the money I offered her as compensation.

That was the beginning of a period of constant, continual revelation for me. I watched as Tutune's appetites for pleasure changed. She became a more willing lover and learned how to truly surrender herself to me, without ever losing the spectacular quality of her orgasms. We played little games, trying to guess how long it would take for me to arouse her before falling on top of her, and sometimes both of us were wrong and she would reach ecstasy before I even penetrated her. Yet for me she was always a sober lover, both in gestures and in words, but her caresses always brought me great pleasure, and sometimes she even reminded me of my sister.

She loved coming to me nude, with no adornments or perfumes, as if to ensure that I loved her for her, for who she was. But there were times when I wanted something more, and she would obligingly accept the diversion: negligees, lace garters, a tiny silver or gold cache-sexe upon the vertical smile between her thighs. At the beginning, out of some kind of odd prejudice, I had imagined that most of the lingerie available in those days would clash with her coal-black skin. But I was utterly wrong: almost everything looked wonderful on Tutune. In the intimate apparel I dressed her in, she seemed less exotic and more accessible, more lusty. She had the kind of foot known as a Greek foot, where the second toe is longer than the big one, and the sole of her foot was exactly the same rosy hue as her labia. Whenever I helped pluck her hairs, I always kissed the spot where a hair had just been uprooted.

I spent days absorbed by the challenge of capturing the light as it fell upon her black skin: the sepia-tinted sheen, the violet shadows. Compared with her, the white skin of the models at school seemed almost childish. The sensual smell of oil and her fiery image conspired exactly as they had years before when I photographed Muriel, and Tutune and I always ended up in bed after each photography session.

I never wanted her more desperately than the times I had to leave her to go to class, although I soon discovered I wanted her even more when I returned to find her at home. She didn't like to be alone, but she didn't like going out for walks either, perhaps because she drew so much attention. When I would run late, she would get bored and go to the brothel, and then I would experience

the torture of jealousy. She was so accustomed to charg-
ing money for sex and making love with many men that
sometimes I worried that she missed her job as a paid
lover. But she said she only went to talk with her girl-
friends, and every time I went to pick her up there she
was, sitting with them. One night when they told me she
hadn't been at the brothel, I waited for her in the attic
and she told me she'd gone to see a Max Linder movie.

To keep her company I bought her a little cat with
orange-colored stripes, and we named him Toulouse. She
was enchanted by him, and even taught him how to lick
her breasts with his rough tongue. When we made love,
Toulouse would inevitably grow agitated and try to join
in, jumping onto the bed and playfully biting our toes.

The armistice day arrived without my having been
called into service, but shortly afterward I was notified that
I was to enlist. I was to be a soldier, second class, in the eigh-
teenth division of military nurses at the base in Bayonne.
Tutune and I would be separated until my first furlough,
which would be granted at the end of four months.

On our last night together we made spectacular love,
as if we had reached the very pinnacle of erotic intimacy
and wisdom, our bodies having learned to harmonize to
the notes of one single melody. Over and over again we
reached new, unexpected peaks of passion, and she moaned
loud and clear, scratching my back instinctively, caught in
the throes of her ecstasy. I was almost afraid to leave now
that I saw I had awakened feelings and needs that she
would be so unable to satisfy by herself.

Tutune didn't know how to read, but we agreed that
I would write to her anyway, and that one of her girl-
friends would read her my letters and then write me back
in her name. Three months went by before I heard from
her, and I sorely regretted not having installed her in some
hotel in Bayonne just to have her nearby. When I returned on leave she was gone, and so were her clothes.
Toulouse was nowhere to be found either, and the mail-
box was stuffed full of letters.

I went to the brothel. Nobody knew anything, nor
had they seen her since I had left. Incredulous, I asked
Madame Ravel if I could inspect the rooms. I went to the
police stations, the hospitals, everywhere. I couldn't believe that Tutune—a woman so used to submitting to
other people's desires—would have decided to leave me,
nor could I believe that she would do so without leaving
any sort of sign. It took me a long time to accept that she
had left voluntarily, so I wouldn't be able to find her, and
it also took me time to realize that people have the right
to love, but they also have the right to leave, disappear,
go away.

More than a year after she left—I had been dis-
charged from the army for some time—I felt something
move in the bed and brush against my face. I woke up, my
heart skipping a beat. I almost thought I heard Tutune's
muffled laugh. But no, it was Toulouse, who had slid toward the window and was now rubbing up against a pillow. I stroked him for a long time and with my emotions
soaring, I listened to his purrs, thinking about how we

had both enjoyed these same pleasures so long ago. I fed him and then he escaped out the window, his tail standing up on end, as if this was part of his everyday routine.

I figured I would see him regularly now, but once again I was mistaken. I consoled myself thinking that perhaps he was somewhere, not too far away, with his mistress, and I prayed that his brief visit was a sign that I had waited long enough, and that she had sent him to bring me some measure of tranquillity and peace.

XII

The Golden Fleece

The combination of pleasure and love is a rare one; when it does occur it tends to be short-lived. More typically we look for pleasure when we are bored by love, and we pursue love when we are tired of physical pleasure. After losing Tutune, I spent many long hours thinking about my father and the Polish woman, and I came to understand why he had worked so hard to cover up the void she created when she died.

I think I must have been going through something akin to heat. If I had been a woman, I swear I would have become a prostitute. And if I had had the slightest notion of seduction, I would have become a gigolo. I can't think of a more sincere or, curiously enough, more honest way to give oneself up to others and earn a living at the same time.

But I was incapable of either of those things, and so I would sit at an outdoor café or on a park bench like a prematurely dirty old man, and stare at the parade of legs that walked past me. With my head bowed, I feigned an ornithologist's interest in the sparrows, crows, and pigeons that fought over the breadcrumbs at my feet as I played a mental guessing game of distinguishing the young virgins from the married women by the shoes they wore, the way they walked, or the length of their skirts. I would lift my eyes only when I had reached my verdict. I wasn't always right, and in any event I never had enough information to know anything for certain, since some young women—virgins or not, I never really knew—wore very provocative shoes that accentuated the arch of the foot, making them sway their hips as if propped up on high heels of two different heights. And some older matrons certainly co-opted the simple, elastic stride of youth, short skirts, and ballet shoes or flat sandals as instruments of seduction.

There were moments when I could stand it no longer, when my fleshy prong fought to pierce my trousers and break through to the light of day, just like an uprooted tree whose roots continue to break through the earth despite the fact that they are no longer needed for support. At those moments I would arise from the bench with more or less dignity depending on the occasion, and run to the brothel. I didn't always arrive in time, and sometimes I didn't even bother trying. If I wore a raincoat or overcoat, my own hands would provide the satisfaction I needed. In the summertime, a light hat, strategically placed and lined with a handkerchief, would give shelter to my release. If anyone glanced over at me, all they would have seen was a self-absorbed young man with sad eyes, insistently stroking the brim of his hat.

After the brothel, the street, and the parks, the thing
that appealed to me the most was the cinema. I remembered that time when Tutune returned to the attic and
told me she had just seen a movie, and though I would
never admit it to myself, I still clung to the hope of finding her in one of those theaters as the lights suddenly went
up. Of course, that was the golden age of silent film, before the powerful and infinite subtleties of the visual image found themselves beholden to the insipid nature of
words. One day I saw *The Madness of Doctor Tube,* and as
I marveled at the truly ominous effects of Abel Gance's
distorted mirrors and trick photography, I finally understood how and why my own, more traditional painting
had long since lost its meaning.

A new model came to pose at the academy: Claire.
The hair on her head was thick and black as a crow's,
while her pubic hair was a brilliant gold, and the other
students and I would argue over which was dyed. Her skin
was extremely pale, and when she posed as one of the
luxuriantly inebriated maenads in Titian's *Bacchanal,* she
would recline backward, remaining as motionless as a sculp-
ture, just as when she posed as Boucher's *Miss O'Murphy,*
stretching out her youthful, plump legs upon the lounge
cushions with unabashed satisfaction. You could just imagine her seeking her release from all those hours of immo-
bile servitude in an explosion of wildly frantic spasms.
She had a boyfriend, a very tall, dreamy-eyed stage actor
named Gérard.

One night as I sipped a glass of wine at a bar on the Place de la Bourse I saw her walk in. She smiled warmly and came over to me.

"Good evening, Pierre," she said. "This should be a moment of great victory for you."

"Good evening, Claire. I'm not certain I understand what you mean."

"You've been wanting me for months, and today I can be yours. I know it won't be as thrilling as if you'd never seen me nude. But I'll do more than pose. I promise."

"Why me?" I asked, stupidly.

"I feel like making love. And you're young and attractive enough. But maybe you'd prefer I look elsewhere."

I left some change on the bar counter and we left. On the way to my house our arms brushed against each other, and she took my hand as I held onto her waist. On the staircase she offered me her carmine-colored lips, and I felt myself sucked into the vortex of her blazing tongue. I had never been kissed like that before; I had never known that a kiss could produce so much pleasure. The stairs gave way beneath us and the entire building seemed to shake.

Her fervor only grew when she saw the mirror. She removed everything but her black stockings and threw me onto the bed. I wanted to continue kissing her and playing with her breasts but she burned with impatience.

"Stick it in!" she whispered in my ear, gripping my neck.

Her lips opened like the petals of a flesh-eating flower and she guided my prick deep down into her moist passageway. But then, suddenly, she stopped, and pressed hard against me so I couldn't possibly escape her embrace. Then she made me turn around and laid me on my back. I reveled in the slick friction of her legs as she perched herself atop the backs of my thighs, raised up her torso, and looked at herself in the mirror, as if posing for herself. Now I was the one having trouble holding back.

"Claire!" I called out.

In a series of syncopated poses, turning her head and bending her torso to one side and then the other, she embarked on the journey to find her rhythm. Her lunges began coming faster and faster, growing increasingly more violent, almost as if she were trying to fly. Her face became transfigured as she let out little cries, like a seagull, and then suddenly she seemed to shrink back. Soon I felt the welcome wave that tightened my thighs and I gratefully surrendered under Claire's pale body. As I ejaculated I saw her eyes open wide, searching for the reflection of my orgasm in her own spectacular image.

She extricated herself from me and together we fell asleep. Some time later I was awakened by her caresses. As Claire groped at my testicles, she kissed the base of my penis, curled her lips around the tip and stimulated the tiny aperture with her tongue, sucking on it. In the mirror her black hair was like the resplendent mane of a wolf.

"What are you doing?" I asked her, although the answer was obvious.

"I'm picturing you as a great big piece of candy," she said, panting.

Her neck stiffened and she closed her mouth around my penis, traveling deeper and deeper until reaching its hilt. Then she withdrew entirely, only to bury me in her mouth one more time. After going through this several more times, my penis began to tremble and I ejaculated. Claire swallowed it all.

As she savored it, she said, "You taste like almond milk." Then, a late-blooming drop of semen emerged on the tip of my penis and she caught it with one of her fingers, drinking in the scent. "And you smell . . . you almost smell like sandalwood. Why do you shave down there?"

I had gotten into the habit of shaving myself when I was living with Tutune, partially out of solidarity and partially out of inclination. And I continued to do the same in Bayonne, as it was a guaranteed way to stave off the lice that seemed to pervade life in the lower ranks of the military.

"The hair on my body," I explained, "has always bothered me. I don't think it's so strange. . . . Cyclists shave their legs, you know."

"You should have left a little tuft, right here," she said, passing her hand across my hairless pubis. "You have very soft skin for a man."

"Not as soft as yours . . ." I said, my eyes trailing down to my waning penis. "And now I can't even show my appreciation, at least not now."

"There are many ways you could show your appreciation," she said, laughing and leaning backward to reveal her sensuous fur.

Beneath her thicket, a myriad of naturally golden hues, her sex was ripe and bulbous. Her fleshy lips throbbed beneath the pressure of my tongue; a shiver raced through my body and a moan escaped from my lips as I savored her, inhaling the sweet aroma of her vulva.

Afterward as we took a brief intermission to rest, I asked her about Gérard. She told me that after living together for three years, he had left her for another woman. That, apparently, was why she had been so bold with me. She was out for revenge and at this point I wasn't sure what number I had been in the succession of Gérard's substitutes.

Whether it was my inborn lust or her affinity for my bedroom mirror, I don't know. But it happened: Claire took Tutune's place in between my legs—though not in my heart—for over a year. Beyond the obvious difference in skin color, the contrast between Claire and her predecessor was striking. During sex, Tutune's mind seemed to focus in on one single point, and she would have a deep, intense orgasm. Claire was more diffuse; her pleasure rippled on endlessly, like a buoy bouncing in the waves of an ocean. She demanded more attention and she recovered more quickly. She was also much more active. She liked to wake me up by sitting on my face, rubbing her sex against my mouth, or masturbating me as she had done the first night, pressing a finger between my testicles and my anus. She had one special idiosyncrasy that I think all curious lovers would do well to add to their repertoire: she was particularly sensitive to caresses behind her knees, and liked me to ride her from behind, like a dog, while she looked into the mirror to observe the metamorphosis of our two-headed monster and the ever-increasing violence of our orgasms.

In general, our relationship was one of innocence teetering on the edge of deviance. One afternoon when I returned from school, I found her kneeling down in bed enduring the attack of a naked man who I soon realized was her ex-lover. Their eyes were wide open, but they were caught in the throes of their mutual passion, and only saw each other in the mirror. I stood there, fascinated by their spasms of pleasure.

"Good afternoon, Claire," I said politely once they were finished. "I'm so glad to see you haven't been missing me."

Two bewildered faces turned toward me.

"Pierre, I didn't hear you come in," she said, regaining her composure. "Have you been here long?"

My response was indifferent, since they hadn't managed to disentangle their bodies quite yet. "The next time you plan to sleep with another man in my bed," I advised her sarcastically, "do be kind enough to warn me in advance, all right?"

"That's exactly what I wanted to talk to you about. Do you know Gérard?" she asked, in an astonishing display of cold blood. "Gérard, this is Pierre."

My presumed rival, who seemed to feel either safer or more comfortable remaining in his position underneath Claire's body, stretched out his hand for me to shake. I began to laugh at the utter cliché of the situation.

"We've seen each other, I think, at the school," I said, as I shook his hand. "And what was it that you wanted to talk to me about?" I asked Claire.

"Gérard and I are getting married."

I felt a slight wave of nausea come over me.

"But you hated him," I protested. "You told me he left you for another woman."

As it turned out, they had reconciled after many long, involved conversations. Claire had been planning to tell me, but he had accompanied her back to my apartment— to avert the possibility of my dissuading her, I suppose— and once they saw the mirror they couldn't resist the temptation. At least that was what they told me. As soon as Claire left with her things, I decided it would be wise to change the lock, to avoid any more surprises in the future.

"There's a big bulge in your pants," Claire observed.

"For God's sake, Claire! What did you think—that I would stop wanting you just like that?"

They carefully extricated themselves from one another. She remained where she was, turning to face me, her elbow raised like Ingres's *Odalisque with a Slave*. Gérard, who also remained lying on the bed, turned away in a rare gesture of discretion.

"Is it me that you desire, or is it us?" asked Claire, looking me straight in the eye.

"You," I said, and I meant it, although there was a tiny part of me that did admire the slender nudity of her boyfriend.

"Come, then," she said, opening her arms. "Gérard isn't a jealous man." And as she saw me hesitate a bit, she added, pointing to the bulge beneath my trousers, "Your best friend has already forgiven me."

Her artlessness was irresistible. I removed my clothes and lay down next to her. Her recent session with Gérard had warmed her up well, and I slid with ease into that little muff of moist flesh, slick and smooth from earlier secretions. What a delight it must be to savor the contrast between the two of us, I thought to myself. I let out a deep sigh and began my long, slow quest for pleasure.

"Oh, yes!" she exclaimed. "How sublime!"

Suddenly I felt the bracing grip of an arm around my chest. It was Gérard, leaning over me from behind. I opened my legs, not terribly scared, for I have always believed that pleasure entails a certain degree of risk. The unsettling caress culminated in pain, but at that moment my slow maneuvers began to rock back and forth with a vengeance and Claire exploded in a paroxysm of gasps and sighs. At the moment of ejaculation, a trickle of saliva fell from my lips. We were one body, with one vulva and two penises, although there were moments when I think none of us was quite sure whether we were one woman and two men or three men or three women.

They invited me to the wedding. I didn't go to the church ceremony but I did go to the party in the evening, in a fourth-floor apartment on the Rue de la Fusterie. Someone I didn't recognize led me to a room filled with guests, and Gérard came over to greet me and offer me a drink, chilled champagne or hot punch. I chose the champagne and asked after Claire.

"She's inside," he said, turning to attend to his other guests. "What a shame you came so late. She would have loved for you to have been among the first."

I watched a pale man exit and another man enter a door to the side of the room. That was when I understood what he meant: as a way of celebrating their nuptials, Claire was offering herself to all her male friends. I looked over at Gérard, who was smiling serenely. How very right she was: this was not a jealous man.

I told him that I was late for another date and handed him my present, a color portrait of Claire in pastels. It wasn't that I was afraid of finding her tired, nor did I feel uninspired by the notion of being one in a long list of men that evening. I just didn't want to wait around for something that only one month earlier, I had had all to myself several times a day.

Claire continued to pose at the École des Beaux-Arts. Somehow, the other students had also discovered that the hair on her head was what she dyed. One day I bumped to her in the cloister. She was radiant with satisfaction.

"Admit it," she bragged. "That there were moments when I made you very happy."

"Moments!" I retorted. "You made me scream with pleasure dozens, maybe hundreds of times."

That was when she admitted to me that while she preferred Gérard's body, my caresses were far superior to his.

XIII

The Battle of the Amazons

I completed my studies at the École des Beaux-Arts with the conviction that I had worked very hard but in the wrong direction. I felt a desperate need to find my own style, one that I could identify with and that would also distinguish me from other painters. I haunted the Musée des Beaux-Arts in Bordeaux, searching for something to admire among the monstrosities there until one day I stopped in front of Delacroix's oil painting of *Greece on the Ruins of Missalonghi*. Suddenly I felt a longing for the *Sardanapalus* in the Louvre—a work so much more powerful than the painting before me. After making a few brief calculations I decided that the money I received from my mother would be enough to cover a short spell in Paris, and I hurried to catch the train.

Those were the days of Carpentier's battles, the arrival of Radiguet, the blossoming of jazz. In a local magazine I read the following sentence signed by Picabia, with which I instantly agreed: "Morality is the backbone of idiots." I attended a Dada demonstration at the Gaveau salon, where a group of playwrights and their friends performed a series of short theater pieces. All the Dadaists were there, with rubber tubing and funnels protruding from their heads, dressed in tablecloths or in ballerina costumes. Breton, whom I recognized from photographs I had seen of him, had glued a pair of revolvers to both his temples. The group's previous demonstrations had been equally outrageous, and that day the public had come prepared with eggs and scraps of meat. The Dadaists responded to the whistles and the deluge of perishable goods with a steady stream of insults until finally the performance was aborted—or perhaps more accurately was transformed into something else entirely, something no less incredible or disgusting.

With slight hesitation, mainly because I was afraid of having nothing to say to him, I visited Max Jacob, who lived on very little means in a tiny house on the Rue Gabrielle on the Montmartre hill. A man of unbridled imagination, he had huge eyes framed by eyebrows that were like two Romanesque arches sketched in charcoal. He dominated the conversation from the start. Though he made a joke out of almost everything he was quite demanding when it came to style. It was obvious that he enjoyed the attentions of young men, though he never came on to me personally. Arm in arm, we walked down to La Mère Anceau, a little tavern where he often lunched with an admirer of his, a tall, thin man about my age with hollowed-out temples who made his living as the clandestine publisher of libertine books with equally libertine illustrations. André Malraux had given him a copy of de Sade's *Brothel of Venice*, which had just been published.

Together, the three of us savored the *navarin* with pota-
toes, a specialty of the tavern, as we traded opinions on the
vilified Marquis. On a piece of brown paper Max sketched
a pencil drawing of me which I lost months later when I
moved to the Rue de Sainte-Catherine. I could see they
wanted to be alone and so I said good-bye to them shortly
afterward. They were working on a new edition of *La pied
de Fanchette,* which Restif de la Bretonne had written in
eleven days, and which Max Jacob was to illustrate.

The brothel on the Rue Monsieur le Prince had
changed its window mannequins, which were now full-
body models with shorter hair, more angular faces, and
a sporty air, wrapped in swaths of gray material from the
tops of their breasts down to their knees, as if in Hindu
saris. Their arms and legs were not made of wax but of
some newfangled substance that was more resistant to the
glare of the lightbulbs, which perfectly imitated the texture of real skin.

Madame Ulianov, however, was exactly the same. I
had the feeling she didn't recognize me, though she welcomed me with the same maternal warmth with which
she had received me on my first visit. I would have been
terribly disappointed when I entered the sitting room had
I not encountered Véronique, but luckily there she was,
sitting on an ottoman, engaged in a friendly conversation
with another girl.

"I like that one, the one in the bright red number."

"A man who knows what he wants," Madame
Ulianov observed, nodding her head.

They had reupholstered the leather on the door that connected the sitting room to the hallway, though they hadn't reinforced the partitions, but nobody seemed terribly bothered by it. Véronique wore a transparent silk *chemise-culotte* with flouncy legs that covered her from her neckline down to the crevice where her thighs met. She took it off and as soon as I removed my own clothes, I began to stroke her tiny, pert breasts, first with my hand and then with my tongue.

"Your caresses are so irresistible," she said.

"Caressing you is irresistible," I replied as my hand slid down her warm belly, toward her lips that opened up like those little Japanese paper flowers that open wide when dropped into water.

Véronique grasped my fluttering member and skillfully introduced it into her tunnel of warm flesh, slowly rocking her pelvis to and fro. Pressed against each other, we moved in unison, as she raised her legs high and wrapped them around my chest. Just before I felt the release of her fluid, a paroxysm of ecstasy shook through my body and I spilled forth in an endless bout of pleasure. I moaned as Véronique continued moving and she didn't stop until my moans subsided. I finally grew quiet and she looked at me skeptically, as if doubting such an exaggerated display of pleasure.

When I announced that I was ready for another round, she laughed and called me naughty, and then separated my legs so that she could nestle between them. Stroking my testicles all the while, she massaged my prick with such force that for a moment I wondered if she was trying to rip it from me entirely, or at least render it useless. But she knew what she was doing, and despite the excesses of our previous round I was soon ready to perform the second movement of our symphony and bring it to a vigorous and energetic finale, along with the unsynchronized accompaniment that came from the adjacent rooms.

"I told you the second time would be better," Véronique told me when we were through.

I then confessed that I thought she hadn't remembered me.

"I never forget my beginners," she bragged.

I stayed on the Rue Orfila near the Père-Lachaise cemetery, and each day I would wander through a different neighborhood. I visited Gustave Moreau's studio because he had been Matisse and Rouault's preferred teacher, and though I admired them both very much I was utterly unprepared for the phantasmagoric, sensual, exalted atmosphere I found inside. The themes of his work, drawn from myth and legend, appealed to me far less than his palette, a wisely composed tableaux of colors which he delicately ground together to achieve unusual hues, pale golds, and reds and blues as brilliant as precious stones. Like me, Moreau was as uninspired by realistic renderings of the world around him and considered nature to be nothing more than a pretext for his enigmatic, lusty dreamscapes.

One day while walking past a dress shop I found myself captivated by the stylized mannequins in the window, all of whom were coated in uniform tones of lacquer. Inside I watched as a refined-looking woman tried on various different hats. Our eyes met, and almost involuntarily I shook my head no. She removed the hat and replaced it with another, searching my eyes for approval. More convinced by this model, I nodded my assent and she gestured for me to wait for her.

She was a flexible, agile woman, and her alluring face moved closer to me as if to kiss me but then suddenly she moved backward, as if she had just realized we didn't know each other. Given what happened afterward, I imagine that this was just one of her tricks for trapping men. She wore a green crêpe-de-chine dress whose edges were embroidered with little gray leaves that matched the color of her eyes. Her name was Danielle. She piled a dozen carefully wrapped packages into my arms and then we left for her house. In the brief intimacy of the taxi, our thighs brushed against each other and she grabbed my knee at each curve we turned.

And then we were in her apartment, sitting on a red velvet sofa. Both of us rested an arm against the back, our hands almost touching. Her dress had risen up a bit, revealing the tops of her silk stockings and lace garters decorated with little satin bows. I tried to look at her face as we chatted, but my eyes kept drifting downward, as if magnetically drawn to her legs. Finally I abandoned all decorum and gazed upon them freely.

"You noticed, didn't you?" she asked. "My garters are new, they're very tight. I'm sure they're leaving terrible marks on my legs. Would you be so kind as to check them for me . . . ?"

I had been with enough women to know that nobody needs help removing garters, but I figured it was as fine a start as any. I kneeled before Danielle and my penis began to thump hopefully as she stretched out her lovely leg. I took hold of one garter and slid it downward, stretching it around her knee so as not to hurt her, calibrating every motion. I stopped at her ankle, leaving the garter dangling like a bracelet, and I was about to take care of the other garter when Danielle, in an indifferent tone, suddenly said:

"And the shoe."

I sighed with joy as I took hold of the heel and slowly tugged at it, downward at first, and then toward me.

"Your feet are so lovely . . ." I murmured in ecstasy. "Your ankles, the curve of your arch . . ."

She stretched out her other leg and repeated the wondrous motion, even more slowly if that was at all possible. She changed position, spreading her knees so that I could lower her thin, silken stockings and linger upon her satin skin.

"Do I have red marks?" she asked as she raised her dress, revealing the black lace border of her fluttering panties. "Look closely. Do you see anything?"

"I don't see any marks," I said.

I had just leaned my head down to kiss the inner face of her moist thighs when suddenly she kicked my bulging groin with the tip of her foot, although she did so gently enough that instead of causing pain, it only aroused me more. I lost my balance and fell back on the floor.

"I'm sorry, Danielle. I thought . . ."

"How dare you abuse my trust," she said sternly, and then her expression softened. "You should be grateful to me for allowing you to take off my garters. . . . Would you mind massaging my calves? My legs hurt from so much walking. There are few things more exhausting than going from store to store."

More and more perplexed, I assumed that she just wanted to play a bit before the main event. Danielle raised her legs, which made her dress ride up even more, and she placed her still-stockinged feet upon my shoulders. Intoxicated and captivated by the proximity and promise of such treasures, I pretended to concentrate on a silky calf, rubbing and caressing it. As her fine panties shifted a bit, I caught a glimpse of her chrysanthemum chestnut and rose-colored petals. Almost without realizing, I stretched out my hand to stroke the tender crevice that was now just within my reach.

Danielle's foot dislodged itself from my shoulder and struck my collarbone, much harder this time.

"What are you doing? How dare you?" she exclaimed. Her seductive pose utterly belied the irritation in her voice. "Or did you think that you could take advantage of me just because I allowed you to see something no man has ever had? What disgusting creatures you are. I will never understand your depravity. I'll just bet you've been dreaming of desecrating my temple with that obscene appendage pointing at me from between your legs."

The interruption of my reverie and the injustice of her comments hurt more than the kick to my collarbone. But I didn't want to lose her; I needed her to salve my desire and so I stood up and asked her forgiveness. Once again, her expression changed.

"I believe you, Pierre, but you have so much to learn if our relationship is to blossom. Now then, I will give you one last chance. Take off my stockings for once and for all. But be careful, don't be insolent now."

I pulled down the transparent hose, took hold of one of her bare legs, and began to kiss the tips of her toes.

"I won't hurt you," I promised her, "and I'll leave the minute you ask me to. But I despise it when people make fun of me."

As she didn't seem convinced by my kind intentions, I let go. Evaluating the situation with a very serious look on her face, she asked me to wait for her for a moment. She left the room and after a short while she returned, wearing a pair of white haute-couture pajamas, also crêpe-de-chine, with embroidered blue flounces and edging. The wide pantaloons opened at the midpoint of her calf bone, and her legs peeked out like those fleshy pistils that emerge from between the silken leaves of a calla lily. Her flat slippers, also white with blue embroidery, had a similar effect: a pale arch peeking out from the confluence of a double tongue.

"You certainly didn't need my help this time," I observed sarcastically.

"Don't be cruel, Pierre," she pleaded as she turned to sit down.

"Me, cruel? You are the one who led me here, brought me to boil several times already, only to refuse me each time. You can't do that to all your men."

"Not all," she replied. "But many of them, yes. I still don't understand how I could have been so mistaken about you. I must have been moving too fast. And perhaps," she suggested, horrified, "perhaps you are not even rich!"

"Rich!" I repeated, and I began to laugh, patting the lapels of my new suit, a quite flattering, superbly cut woolen suit which I had bought the day before on sale.

I told her of my limited finances, my fascination with painting, my life in Bordeaux. Then I began to tell her about Muriel, with all the emotions that bubbled up as I remembered her, so far away and after so many years. And there, sitting in the house of a woman I didn't know, I thought of Muriel and I thought of my mother, and I thought of Tutune, and of the many women I had desired and made love to in my life. And then, suddenly, I began to cry. There were so many desirable women in the world, but they were so very difficult to attain. . . . And what could a man do with such an inexhaustible source of desire? Renounce it, immolate oneself voluntarily?

"I would still desire you, even if I were castrated," I told her.

Danielle was touched by my fitful confessions, and she also noted that I was still aroused. There was no hiding it: the confession of my doubts and emotions had not caused my erection to subside.

"I want to see you," she said. "But move back a little, don't come any closer."

I obeyed her and pulled out my stiff penis. Danielle smiled.

"You can do it if you want, over there on the parquet."

I massaged it as I caressed her with my eyes: the way her breasts filled out the blouson of her pajama, the fine weave of the fabric that cloaked her warm fur that my hand had only just tried to stroke. My entire body shook as she crossed and uncrossed her legs, and a thunder continued to rage inside my head that I could no longer ignore. Aware of the immense seductive power of her movements, Danielle shifted her weight onto one of her slippers, her body balancing briefly upon the tip of her toe. My knees buckled and my neck cracked, tilting backward like a wounded beast as my penis finally found its release.

Danielle arose, ensured that my gratifying eruption had not reached the rug, then offered me a glass of cognac. Inspired by the personal secrets I had just revealed to her, she confessed that she made a living from her relationships with men, something I had already suspected. But she despised having to be intimate with them. And so, to fulfill her professional ambitions without getting too close, she had focused on a very specific type of man, the kind that lacked the usual presumptuous virile superiority, the kind that enjoyed being tempted, subjected, and humiliated by a seminude beauty. And contrary to what I thought, there were plenty of men that fit this category, the majority of whom were men in positions of power. She told me about one middle-aged millionaire, for example, whom she would insult as she "shook his big awful thing"—that is, masturbated him—with a silk scarf. And she told me of a certain young man who stood to inherit a tremendous fortune whose only desire was to remove her lingerie. She would then punish him with a slap every time his fingers brushed against her skin.

But she was tired of the millionaire and the young man and was looking for someone, perhaps less insistent, but who felt the same admiration for her. Misled by the smart cut of my suit, she had also been confused by the fact that I had not immediately unbuttoned my pants when I spied her fleshy pink lips. She seemed sincere enough, but I still sensed that she was hiding something from me, and I asked her if she was certain about her aversion to men. She smiled affectionately at the tiny ray of hope that shone through my question.

"Absolutely," she said simply. "I like women."

She told me she had a lover, a woman she went to every night, as if to purify herself after servicing the man of the moment.

I had always been drawn to the idea of watching two—or more—women making love. I had heard that some brothels staged lesbian spectacles, but I didn't have much faith in those passionless performances, conceived only to titillate the tourists.

I told Danielle that if she would allow me to attend one of her erotic interludes she could impose whatever conditions she wished. At first she was outraged; those interludes were far too intimate, she said. But one of the great wonders of the libertine life is the power it holds over people, and the idea of showing me the dazzling beauty of female lovemaking grew on her. Her relationships with her clients were quite masochistic in nature, and so I suppose she had actually begun to enjoy tormenting them on some level. And so she established two conditions: one, that I was prohibited from intervening no matter what my state of arousal, and two, that her companion would have to consent.

We went to a building on the Rue Barbusse, near the Luxembourg Gardens. I waited anxiously at the foot of the staircase, and after a short while I was invited upstairs. I watched everything from a seat in the hallway as I was expressly prohibited from stepping inside the bedroom.

It was quite a performance, a battle between two amazons with round, turgid breasts and immense strong thighs. They allowed themselves not even a moment of rest, each one intent upon wrenching the greatest number of orgasms possible from the other. Amid a chorus of insistent howls, their bodies arched back as they tangled and contorted themselves into a labyrinth of flesh. It was such an intense tornado of passion that if a bolt of lightning had crashed through the room I wouldn't have been the least bit surprised.

I was forbidden from joining them, but nothing had been said about liberating my pulsating member from the confines of my trousers. I took it out and grabbed it urgently.

As my back shook spasmodically and my gaze focused on the struggle between a pointy breast and a vulva, I thought of the breasts and vulvas I had seen in Gustave Moreau's studio, and I suddenly had a vision: paintings of intertwined couples, creatures with long, shiny legs, lusty sphinxes copulating with open-lipped sirens. Torture-inducing fingernails and stocking seams, seams in bold relief, like long, endless scratches. A myriad of jade tones passed through my mind, as did the cadences of amber and mother-of-pearl, the opaline sheen of semen. I wanted to paint seductive monsters with bold bursts of enamel.

I spilled forth my desire. I had finally found my style. Now all I had to do was create the painting.

XIV

The Physiology of Marriage

The works I envisioned were far bigger than any I had ever painted before, and so I moved to an apartment at number 9 Rue de Sainte-Catherine, the same apartment where I write these words: an attic with a bathroom, kitchen, and five bedrooms, one of which is large enough to serve as my studio. At first I missed the diminutive scale and cosiness of my old attic flat, but I was still close to the Place de la Bourse and I could visit the fountain of the Three Graces whenever I wished.

I soon discovered it was no easy task to render on canvas those veritably pyrotechnic wonders I had envisioned while watching the erotic battles between Danielle and her friend. Progress was exasperatingly slow but sure, and my work began to take shape around the same time the Bordeaux artistic scene was beginning to loosen up. The Salon d'Automne, which was the most retrograde of them all, had allowed the exhibition of some moderately abstract canvases, and the Salon des Dessinateurs was showing works by Marie Laurencin, Max Jacob, and Francis Picabia. The Bordeaux Society of Independent

Artists was founded around that time, and its main objective was to inaugurate an annual salon that would be open to any and every artist who wished to participate. I exhibited a few of my earlier pieces since I was still working on my newer ones, and was amused to see how both the public and the local critics encouraged me to continue down a path that I had long since abandoned.

Regarding my wife, I have very little to say. Our differences were not entirely her fault—after all, I must acknowledge my own immoderate lust and the restrictions of marriage itself, which I have always felt should be preceded by a trial period. Balzac once said—and I think he would still defend the point—that of all the institutions known to humanity, none has progressed less than that of matrimony.

I met Lucie in the Salon des Indépendants. Someone told her that I had talent, and in an attempt to seem bold and insouciant in front of her friends, she approached me for an autograph. She was a dark-skinned girl with a pointy chin and a heart-shaped face, and she gazed at me with friendly interest as I handed back the catalogue with my signature. She half closed her eyes and then suddenly opened them wide, as if trying to show me that my image was now imprinted on her brain, or that anything was possible as long as the two of us were together. Shortly afterward I learned that she was nineteen years old, that she came from a wealthy family, and that her father was a councilman in the city government. None of this dissuaded me. I invited her to my apartment.

I showed her the salon, the room where I stored my paintings, my disorganized studio. As soon as we reached the bedroom, I grabbed her and kissed her. She made no objections. As I wrapped my arms around her neck, she pressed against me, luxuriating in the kiss. My member stood guard and pressed into her thigh, searching for shelter.

With this same, natural ease I helped her out of her jacket and tucked her into the same bed I am lying in now. I laid down at her side, kissing her all the while. I began to unbutton her blouse to caress her neckline, her breasts, and in the giant horizontal mirror I saw someone who looked like me, a rival who seemed intent upon making every last effort to rip her away from me.

"Why don't you take the whole blouse off, that way it won't wrinkle," Lucie said, sitting up.

Underneath she wore a lilac-colored corselet with a matching lace border and hooks and eyes down the front. I slowly undid the clasps, kissing her, licking her, and pressing my lips against the tiny orbs that had not quite reached maturity but which were already endowed with generous, highly sensitive nipples. My devious hand slid down toward the waistline of her dress, insistently trying to explore and eliminate any further obstacles. That was when Lucie grabbed me by the neck.

"You can keep kissing me," she warned, "but don't touch me there."

I feigned resignation and resumed work on her nipples and her lips in the hope that one of these two areas would transmit the powerful incandescence of desire to the other. I repeated the tactic several times, but with no luck. Finally, Lucie explained to me that she was a virgin and that she intended to remain that way until she married. She was convinced that she should be intact on her wedding day, and that her husband would consider it a necessary prerequisite, given her social class. In vain I tried to convince her of how absurd it was to renounce such an extraordinary pleasure to satisfy such an ordinary convention, and I also told her that if her husband really loved her he would hardly care about the absence of a tiny, two-millimeter membrane. She admitted to me that she too found such conventions maddening, but she also felt that those who disobeyed them would invariably end up in solitude and misery. In any case, she pointed out, there were other ways of achieving pleasure.

"With other women?" I asked her, thinking of Danielle.

"No, no. That sort of thing doesn't appeal to me." And with calculated audacity she added: "I prefer the male body."

"If you wish," I offered, "I could show you one right now."

"I'd rather you kept on kissing me."

"But what for, if I can't go any further? I don't understand—what is this other method of achieving pleasure?"

"I give it to myself," she whispered after a long pause, as if confessing a horrible sin. "Stop! What are you doing?"

"I want to show you what you are missing."

I unzipped my pants and displayed my jewels in all their pulsating glory.

"My goodness!" she exclaimed, her eyes opening wide. "There is no way that such a thing could ever fit inside my body. Have you seen its head? My God, and its length is positively monstrous. Pierre, you never should have shown it to me."

"I assure you it is perfectly designed to fulfill its objective."

"It must be very painful," she whispered weakly.

"Don't be afraid; it can only bring you pleasure."

My penis was about to explode, and almost imperceptibly I shook it a tiny bit, which only precipitated the finale. Lucie got up and began to run toward the hall. As I ejaculated, I called out her name, and my last few spasms were accompanied by the sound of the staircase door closing.

I still don't understand why I insisted upon pursuing her. I found out her telephone number, made several dates with her, and we went out a number of times. The rules were always the same, and it seemed that seeing my member only confirmed her convictions: caressing her from the waist down was strictly prohibited. One day, Lucie told me that I was putting her in a compromising position and that we either had to formalize our relationship or end it altogether. I ignored the warning and decided to meet her family, who confirmed my worst suspicions in the areas of piety and conservatism. But thanks to the property my mother possessed I was not considered an unworthy option. Suddenly, I surprised myself by bringing up the subject of marriage.

And that was how I, a man who listens to Sunday masses on the radio for a bit of a laugh, committed the hypocritical act of getting married in a cathedral, with all the pomp and circumstance befitting a councilman's daughter. My mother wrote us a warm, affectionate letter, and apologized for her absence claiming health problems. I almost thanked her for not coming, because my feelings for her were still so strong. And although Lucie wanted to visit her on our honeymoon, I persuaded her that we should go to Paris instead.

Our wedding night was a bit trying. My dazzling wife was mortified by the insertion of my penis. It was useless for me to insist that, in fact, I was of rather average size: since she had nobody to compare me with, she did not believe me for a second. And so I had to settle for a painfully prolonged distension, as laborious as a surgical operation. I had wanted her for so long, with a desire of such great magnitude and imagination, that fulfilling the desire was a letdown. It was difficult to actually believe that I had finally possessed her. I began to sense that no matter how many thousands of times I went to bed with Lucie, I would never really possess her as fully as I had hoped.

That very night, as soon as she fell asleep, I began to deceive her. I didn't even go looking for Véronique. On the Rue Lapp, I hired two of those mercenary girls who had accosted me on my first visit to Paris, and I took them to a pension. In the hours that followed my hands massaged and caressed breasts, asses, and mounds of soft fur. I reveled in ecstasy four times.

Relations with Lucie did not improve in the days that followed. I broke her hymen and widened her opening, but I couldn't deny it: my dazzling wife still retained a trace of prudishness and though she did surrender to me, she did so with reservations. Oddly enough, she never stopped asking me to kiss her. She would speak of her love for me, of my egotistical pleasure-seeking, of my lack of romance.

"But this," I exclaimed, administering a lascivious fondle, "is what romance is!"

Despite her declarations, Lucie was not truly obsessed with the male form, at least not in the way I was with the female body. Nor did she have much imagination, or tolerance, or any capacity for admiration. Upon seeing the *Sardanapalus,* all she said was that she found it rather large. Like my penis.

We did have some happy moments when we returned to Bordeaux. Love inspires a desire for shared happiness, and Lucie, who did love me in her own way, displayed an exaggerated kind of affection whenever she saw me pick up my paintbrushes. She would enter the studio and kiss my neck and whisper all sorts of flattery, interrupting my flow of concentration. But never did she show any real interest in my paintings or make any genuine attempt to encourage my efforts. To put an end to her constant interruptions, I had to install a deadbolt on the door.

Not long afterward, she became pregnant. Her contours changed as her feminine form blossomed, grew more abundant, and her breasts grew large round areolas. She was never more beautiful than she was during those first four or five months of pregnancy, nor was she ever so passionate. One night I convinced her to allow me to slide my penis between her breasts, and though she was reluctant she relented, for she knew the pleasure it gave me. And then she changed again: in her seventh month she asked me to stop making love to her until the baby came.

She gave birth to a lovely little girl, whom we baptized Muriel. Lucie placed her crib in our bedroom, and whenever I would try to make love to her she would say she wasn't fully recovered from the childbirth. Occasionally she would agree to relieve me with her hands but her lack of both desire and technique frustrated my own pleasure. I began to have fantasies of abusing her. I pictured myself slapping her, pressing her face against the pillow, and ripping off her lingerie to reveal the rippled mound that was so forbidden to me. I pictured myself penetrating her with my fingers until she was wide open and moist, and then I would grab the back of her neck as I introduced my erect member (which acquired mythical proportions in these fantasies) into her orchid of flesh.

As a consequence of these daydreams I returned to Madame Ravel's brothel and had a brief affair with a married woman. I would also bring models home, locking myself away with them in my studio to fornicate on a divan.

You can never truly know a woman until you betray her. Whenever I would bring a model home for sex, Lucie would pretend not to hear our shouts of pleasure, and she remained silent about the situation.

Of course, it was all merely an effort to attract her attention, to make her desire me as much as I desired her. One day, in bed, I watched as her nightgown rose up while she slept, and lay there admiring her ass: the smooth, dimpled skin, the gracefully turgid cheeks, and the little nub, as fleshy as the crater of a tiny asteroid. Suddenly a violent, voluptuous wave of desire rocked through me and I knew that no force on earth would be able to stop me from exploring that slender path.

I laid down on Lucie's back, resting the weight of my body on my elbows and knees, and I guided my penis's bulging head toward that fleshy nub—it felt like two tiny lips delicately kissing my member. My wife woke up, looked at me over her shoulder, and began to scream. I pressed on and the narrow opening gave way.

Just as I had done in my fantasies, I pushed her face into the pillow and rode her as her screams grew louder. The baby woke up and began to cry, but the element of perversity in that pleasure made it utterly uncontrollable. Lucie's ass quivered beneath my belly.

The next day, she and baby Muriel left me.

XV

The Mirrored Room

Since I didn't make a living from my paintings and was in fact my own main client, I could allow myself the luxury of working at my leisure. I didn't complete my series of five massive canvases until 1936: *Succubus, Omphale, Pentesilea, The Battle of the Amazons,* and *The Warrior Women*—five brilliant tableaux of naked bodies making the most savage, feverish kind of love with members of either their own or the opposite sex.

The directors of the Salon des Indépendants were shocked. They didn't know how to react to paintings whose size, crude themes, and liberal painterly treatment rendered them so disturbing and so very different from my earlier works.

"You've succumbed to the temptation of abstraction," one of them sharply accused me, with the disdainful tone of someone who felt personally betrayed.

"Nonsense," I declared. "If I had wanted to create abstract paintings, I would have done it—you wouldn't even have known where the skin began and where it ended. The real problem is that you are a bunch of puritans, and you can't bear the eroticism that flows from my canvas."

The very standards established by the Indépendants—that of maintaining an exhibition open to all—would not allow them to ban my work. The day the show opened, scandal broke out in the public courtyard. The city government, the prefecture, and a few local organizations declared their disgust most vociferously. They all appealed to the president of the Société des Indépendants, who had never liked me much. The visitors to the exhibition would walk right past the other paintings, only to form little clusters around mine.

"Look, that's it, that's the penis, right there," one woman exclaimed to another, pointing with her parasol. "What a lack of decorum! And that thing sticking out of her behind. . . . It can't be! It . . . it looks like a vibrator. . . ."

Feigning great chagrin, the president informed me that I would have to withdraw my paintings.

"But why?"

"Well . . . because . . . after all . . ." And with poorly concealed irritation he pointed to *Succubus*. "It is eminently clear that that man right there is sodomizing her."

"Are you sure it's a man? And that the other one is a woman? After all, weren't you the ones who said I had become too abstract?"

They threatened to pull all the other painters' works if I didn't voluntarily withdraw my own, and they did just that, piling all the paintings up against a wall. They

were more than prepared to shut down the exhibition
entirely, but then I suggested they simply cover up my
paintings. Delighted, they agreed. "If you cover them we
won't close down," they said.

We found some wide canvas dropcloths and hung
them in front of my paintings. Next to them I placed a
small sign calling the exhibition organizers censors and a
bunch of fake Indépendants. Once again, they withdrew
the other paintings in protest. I, in turn, crossed out the
parts of the message that most offended them, and they
relented, reopening the exhibit. It was quite a comedy and
actually rather entertaining. The visitors to the exhibit
would lift up the dropcloths to look at my work and
struggle to read the parts I had stricken from my warning sign. I would hide behind a group of planters and
warn the viewers who approached: "You know, they
covered those pieces because they were painted with
semen. . . . The Indépendants don't like paintings made
with semen."

The first blow was delivered by a certain well-known
critic who wrote in *Sud-Ouest* that I was like the painter
Frenhofer in Balzac's "Le chef d'oeuvre inconnue," a man
who works and searches so long and so hard that he be-
gins to question the very object of his search. According
to the critic, my delirium had led me to despise Beauty—
which he had written just like that, capitalized—and my
work had become a kind of shapeless fog, an extravagant
melee of lines and colors. Of this monumental mess, he
declared, the only thing worth mentioning was a tiny

corner of one of the paintings—he couldn't remember which one, since it was all such a jumble in his mind— "the marvelous and inimitable shape of a foot bound in a fishnet stocking, as real as life itself."

I didn't know whether to thank him for the praise or challenge him to a duel.

Games aside, the exhibit and the article sealed my destiny in many ways, because the other critics wasted little time in launching into their own Balzac comparisons. Artistically as well as socially I found myself forced to forge my path on the margins of what was considered acceptable. The bourgeois arbiters of taste turned their backs on me, saying they understood perfectly why Lucie had had to leave me.

The following year I once again made the front page of the local papers with what came to be known as the "Three Graces scandal." One night the police found me drunk in the Place de la Bourse, making love to one of the permanently wet statues in the fountain, and they arrested me on the spot. I spent ten days in jail and was issued a fine for disturbing the peace. Either my inborn lechery or the effects of alcohol convinced me that I had achieved my goal and that the bronze flesh of the Grace in question had gladly welcomed my ebullient homage. Ever since then there was always some inevitable passerby who, upon seeing me, would inevitably mutter: "That's the statue pervert."

I suppose that episode was the culmination of a progressive isolation that had begun with Lucie's departure.

My first night alone, without her and without our child, I rummaged through her drawers, still filled with her things. My wife had left with a small suitcase, figuring I would send the rest of her belongings, or that a friend would come by to collect them. Just as I had done so many years earlier in the château, I hunted through the heady profusion of transparent silk chemises, panties with plunging décolletage, and suggestive pajamas. They were all an allusion to a kind of pleasure I had so rarely enjoyed with her, and suddenly those pleasures became as vivid as if I had only just lost them.

I sensed that I would miss her less, or that her absence would at least become more bearable, if I reincarnated her somehow. I put on a pair of black stockings and a light-pink velvet negligee with red sable trim that ran around the neckline and all the way down the front opening to the seam at the knee. It would have been impossible—for anyone but Lucie, that is—to wear those bits of lingerie and not feel unbearably aroused. I observed myself in the mirror and watched as the head of my penis peeked out naughtily from the front opening of the negligee. I wanted to put on lipstick, a hat, or a turban to add some kind of realism to the vision, but I didn't make it in time. My hand took care of the rest.

Later, in a calmer state, I improved the scenario by adding an infinite number of details, though each one could have renewed my desire on its own. Finally, filled with a sense of plenitude that I hadn't felt for some time, I fell onto the bed and marveled at how those moments of pleasure were in no way inferior to the pleasures I had received at the hands of women. In the end, nobody knows you better than you know yourself.

I also thought about the thousands of cities in the world, filled with women who deserve to be loved, and how improbable it was, in the real world, for a man to ever meet the one woman that is most appropriate for him. A man could risk madness if he tried to possess them all. And it occurred to me that by myself I could assemble all the most seductive qualities of each woman that ever appealed to me, and that I could revel in them all just as I had reveled in Lucie's lingerie. The orgasm, I mused, is so intimate an experience that it doesn't need to be shared with others at all. And I had the time, the predilection, and the space for it. It wasn't the first time for me, anyway: I had once been with a woman with whom I found I needed a bit of encouragement, and she agreed to make up my face, dab me with perfume, and lend me her jewelry.

I decided to consecrate a room to these delights. I sealed the window shut, lined it with red velvet, and out-fitted the entire room with mirrors, even on the door. I told the delivery men who came to install them that I was looking for a new style of painting.

XVI

Le Chevalier d'Eon

Neither the work I dedicated to those paintings nor the limited comprehension with which they were received justified my continued efforts, but I didn't regret painting them. There they were, and together they represented the most important thing I had ever done in my life, though only I was able to truly appreciate them and understand the point to which they reflected my vision. In a much smaller format, but still employing the style that I now call my own, I painted several ghostly, imaginary landscapes. And in the mirrored room I painted myself dressed as a woman, in stockings and high heels, with a dark background flecked with spots of light that perfectly accentuated the color of my skin and my transparent clothes.

I had procured a certain erotic encyclopedia, mainly for its copious illustrations, and on one of its pages I discovered Georges de la Tour's double portrait of the enigmatic historical figure known as the Chevalier d'Eon. On the left side, d'Eon stands bathed in the metallic shimmer of a black mane and the green cape of a *capitan de dragons,* and to the right he boasts a highly feminine dress, with a jaunty pair of nipples peeking out from its square neckline. The terse accompanying text was in German, a language the Christian Brothers had taught me as a young boy, though with only mediocre results. As I read on, I learned that Charles-Geneviève-Louis-Auguste-André-Timothée de Beaumont d'Eon had been born in a small town in lower Burgundy in 1728, and that after being known as a man for forty-six years, he had lived for another thirty-six as a woman until his death in London. D'Eon served as the inspiration for the academics who would later baptize this affinity as Eonism, a persistent, if not uncontrollable, urge to dress up as a member of the opposite sex.

I had neither the intention nor the fear of undergoing such a radical transformation. I, myself, only cross-dressed occasionally, for pleasure, but was so intrigued by the story that I went to the Bordeaux public library in search of more information. The library, though an excellent archive, had not a single work dedicated to the Chevalier in its overloaded bookshelves. Once more I was forced to travel to Paris to satisfy my curiosity.

It was there, beneath the nine glass-domed cupolas of the reading room in the Bibliothèque Nationale, that it first occurred to me to write a novel inspired by the exploits of that amphibious subject, a novel that might strive for the same carefree narrative found in the pages of *Les onze mille verges.* I located a copy of *The Letters and Memoirs of the Chevalier d'Eon,* as well as the voluminous autobiographies of Casanova and Beaumarchais, both of which made mention of the Chevalier, and also found several other period books on transvestitism, such as *The Transvestite Memoirs and the Story of the Marquise-Marquis de Bonneville.* Unlike the others, this one had no literary pretensions whatsoever, and seemed to want nothing more than to shock, scandalize, and entertain any and all potential readers.

Each day I would go to the library, take notes for five or six hours, and walk past the heart of my beloved Voltaire, hidden somewhere inside his bust. Then I would go to Madame Ulianov's brothel, or I would visit Danielle. Despite her lack of desire, she did feel a certain affection for me, and as a special favor she would allow me to join her for the massages she always received following her afternoon nap. Naked, she would lie down upon a cot that was covered in a thin, waterproof black rubber material, and her maid would coat her body in a sweet-smelling oil. My friend would tremble with pleasure as they caressed her breasts, her delicate belly, her slick thighs.

Then, the maid would brush her fingertips across the soft lips nestled beneath Danielle's curly thicket, tickling them expertly as I would violently exhume my apoplectic member from beneath my pants. Once it was time for exercise, the maid would introduce her lubricated index finger into the far reaches of Danielle's vagina, asking her to raise or lower the pressure. As it came out, the impertinent finger would pose, almost nonchalantly, upon Danielle's clitoris, and my friend's legs would quiver in an orgasm that I would try to match with my own, and which served as a kind of aperitif to even greater pleasures.

One afternoon, the session went on longer than usual. I lay down in Danielle's appointed place and this time the maid removed her own clothes as well. She oiled me and then laid me down on my belly before settling down upon me, stretching her body from one end of my back side to the other. A moan escaped my lips from the sheer voluptuous pleasure of feeling those tender breasts rubbing up and down my skin, and that soft, spongy thicket pressing against my ass. She commanded me to turn around, straddling me and massaging me with her entire body from her breasts down to her thighs, not stopping for even a moment of rest. Certain of the effect, she slowly introduced her fingers into our dance. I would try to catch her between my hands but she would always slide away, laughing as she clung to my penis. My paroxysms were so strong I could see them illuminate her face as she felt the spasms.

Danielle told me that occasionally, to both calm and torment the men who desired her, she would make them have sex with her maid. When I told her about d'Eon and my own inclinations, she said that my case was far from unusual. In her experience, most men, even those who seemed so archetypically masculine, adored dressing up as women. She didn't know why, nor was she very interested in questioning it; she assumed it had to be some kind of desire to feel close to women, or to replace them in some way. Cunt envy, she called it. She told me of a very renowned financial executive (she offered no more details) who came to see her quite frequently, only to put on her lingerie, still warm from her body. And then he would ejaculate into her panties while looking intensely into her eyes.

Once I felt that I had gathered all the information I needed from the library, I went to say good-bye to Danielle, who gave me the most marvelous gift: two small gold pendants attached to tiny rings which I could affix to my nipples and which, according to her, heightened sensitivity tremendously during orgasm.

I worked on my book for a year and a half. Contrary to what I had originally thought, the Chevalier d'Eon had not undergone an overnight transformation at all. In fact, his cross-dressing habit went all the way back to his childhood. As a secret agent for Louis XV's clandestine diplomatic missions, he had dressed up as a woman in order to gain the favor of the Russian czarina Elizabeth. Then, pretending he had a sister identical to him, he returned to the Russian court, this time as secretary to the embassy. An able swordsman, he was a *capitan de dragons* in the Seven Years' War and plenipotentiary minister in England, where people placed heavy bets regarding his true gender. Fallen from grace, he was permitted to return to France under the condition that he was never to wear men's clothes again. The surgeon who performed the autopsy discovered a perfectly formed penis and set of testicles. Those are the basic facts. From that point of departure, my novel takes off: a playful, irreverent story that employs a difficult but effective mixture of eroticism and humor. Incidentally, I am not altogether certain that the Chevalier d'Eon was a true Eonist, as the sexologists claim. I tend to think of him more as a dispassionate person who used his skill as a transvestite to achieve his goals in the realms of politics and intelligence.

Sometimes I found I grew so aroused by the things I wrote that I couldn't continue. I would get up, hunt for the bits of lingerie I had either pilfered from Lucie's closet or bought in shops under the flimsiest subterfuge, and I would carefully make up my face, add a necklace and bracelets, decorate my nipples with the little pendants Danielle had given me, bind my chest in a corset, slide my legs into a pair of fishnet stockings, and place a pair of high heels with open toes on my feet. Although I was close to forty years old, I still had a very slender waist and not an ounce of fat on my body. In front of a mirror, at least, I could easily pass for a woman. My pectorals had developed in such a way that from a certain distance and with a necklace and corset in place, my décolletage fooled the eye and was downright seductive.

By the time I would enter the mirrored room, I was generally so worked up that I scarcely had time to admire my costume, but when I managed to contain myself for a few minutes I would grow lightheaded from the immense pleasure I felt, and sighs of admiration and desire would escape my lips. Little tremors would shake through my body, and I would whisper names of women I didn't know, just as I had done so long ago as an adolescent, or I would exclaim again and again in a feigned female voice: "I love you, I love you!" before exploding in murmurs and prolonged gasps that would culminate in a "That's it!" in a shameless, unmistakably male voice.

It's strange: whenever I dressed up as a woman and masturbated, it never felt like masturbation. It felt like sex.

I finished *Le Chevalier d'Eon* in April of 1939. They say that erotica always finds its readership, and I had little trouble finding an editor. It was to be published in September. The five-thousand copies of the first edition were already printed when the Nazis, in their never-ending affinity for oppression, invaded Poland.

XVII

The Ambiguous Woman

The war we were suddenly entangled in, and for which our military leaders were sorely unprepared, did not help to calm my tempestuous soul. I was assigned to the medical outfit of a light infantry division based in Montbard, and when they captured me there, I suddenly found myself part of the amorphous mob of conquered soldiers. Now that they had France under their control, the Germans figured they could do without me and I was sent home.

Bordeaux had been bombed, and the mayor declared himself fascist. Everyone had adjusted to the sudden defeat. In a letter, my mother announced to me that she would now be sending me less money; the invading armies had seized the château's wine cellar. And as far as *Le Chevalier d'Eon* was concerned, I never laid eyes on a single copy. Apparently they would have a difficult time selling it, and with the shortage of raw materials, they finally decided to destroy the books to make cardboard. What a shame: the publication of that book couldn't have been more appropriate than at that moment, when ideological cross-dressing was at its height.

My first painting during those dark years was *The Explosion,* in which I used a wild spray of colors shooting toward the edges of the canvas to represent the effect of a bomb that had been dropped on the neighborhood of Chartrans. One afternoon a German official with a group of armed soldiers under his command appeared at my front door. They carried out a routine search and then a short, chubby general walked in. He wanted to see my paintings. He spoke very good French, with the exception of a few gender errors. I showed him my studio and the room where I stored my canvases, which he examined one by one. When he would find something he liked, he would nod his head.

"How much do you want for these two?" he asked, pointing to *Succubus* and *The Warrior Women.*

I explained that they meant quite a bit to me, and that I wasn't interested in selling them.

"If that is the case, then, I will have to confiscate them," he said.

I realized that no amount of blustering on my part would stop him from confiscating them. I offered him a few other paintings in place of the ones he wanted. I showed him some cracks in dark corners, trying to suggest that the paintings were decaying. I had no idea where he planned to hang them, but I nevertheless claimed they were too big for him. I even showed him the moth-eaten stretcher.

"Please, don't press the issue," the general advised, with his measured, calm tone of voice. "I could make you report immediately to the Forced Labor Program of Germany. Are you a homosexual, sir?"

"My entire body of work is a paean to women," I said, recovering the German of my childhood days as if by magic. "You can see that. All you have to do is look at my paintings."

"This one as well?" he said, pointing to the self-portrait in which I was dressed up as a woman.

"All of us wear some kind of costume. If I were to put on your uniform," I asked, gazing pointedly at his insignias, "would that make me a general in the German army?"

He studied me with a stern face and then began laughing.

"No," he replied, "but then we would have you shot for spying."

They took my paintings. As he left, the general's gaze lingered upon a long-haired wig hanging from the back of a chair.

"Your friend," he said, reverting to French, "must be very lovely."

Sometimes I wonder where those paintings are—that is, if they weren't destroyed during the war—and sometimes I fantasize about how and why an enemy general would have heard of and come to appreciate my works, which had so few admirers, even in my own milieu.

The ambiguous woman appeared at my apartment one day in an Astrakhan coat and a hat that hid her face down to her painted, heart-shaped lips. Even had she not arrived saying that she had an idea to propose to me, I would have invited her in. She smelled like Aphrodisia by Fabergé, a perfume that I had used for my own comfort and solace in better times. And though she refused to remove her coat, claiming she was chilly, I could see the seams of her black stockings dividing each leg into two dizzying lengths of silken flesh. She strode decisively into the salon, as if she had been there before, and sat down on a sofa. She had an exotic accent, which was surprisingly warm and sounded ever so slightly affected.

She asked me if I had any drawings or watercolors of an erotic nature. I showed her what I had on hand, a few sketches on canvas and cardboard that I had used as studies for my five great paintings.

"They are truly magnificent," she said. "But I would prefer something on paper. I don't have the space to hang these. And I'm looking for something more explicit."

The high heels of her shoes stretched out like long needles, and when she crossed and uncrossed her legs I could almost hear the thrush of her black stockings brushing against each other.

"Are you asking me to paint something for you?" I asked her.

"I'll pay you well, of course."

Beneath the veil, I sensed the watchful gaze of an extremely pale face. My finances had been relatively tight recently, and I was suddenly inspired by the idea of satisfying the desires of such a refined woman. I asked her what she meant by something more explicit, and the exotic accent grew stronger and stronger as she explained her idea. She wanted drawings of women dressed in plumed helmets, black corsets, long gloves, garter belts, stockings, and shiny high-heeled shoes. She wanted them to be making love, or locked in a trance state from being whipped or tied by other women, who were to be similarly outfitted.

"I always thought this sort of thing appealed much more to men than to women," I replied.

"Men," she declared, "only know what women allow them to see."

We agreed on a price and a delivery date, and as she left I felt like the lone shipwreck victim who spies a ship in the distance and watches it pass him by at the moment he thinks he's been sighted.

After testing several different methods, I decided on pen and ink. I drew women dressed in black from head to toe, laced up like horses in a funeral procession, tied up and chained to posts, crosses, trees, wheels, torture racks, their eyes blindfolded or wide open with panic, a mixture of interchangeable dominatrixes and slave girls caught in the act of imposing discipline with their breasts or their asses, or with scars etched deep from dozens of previous whippings. There were times when I didn't know whether I was working for the ambiguous woman or for myself. As I idly wondered who she was, I dreamed of her posing for my drawings or growing aroused while admiring them, and I would feel myself become hard and then pour forth my own personal toast to her health.

She would come to collect them, always punctual, always veiled, and always at night. She would study them, make suggestions and comments, pay me, and leave. The sketches she liked the best were the ones that showed no flesh at all, only a few accessories floating in the air like suggestive little mementos. I thought of the mysterious stranger who had commissioned Mozart to compose a requiem shortly before he died, and I wondered if all my erotic accessories and those hollow Venuses were not also related somehow to the cult of the dead, and if they weren't some kind of omen of my own imminent end.

One night, while we looked at the sketches together, I touched her thigh, almost without realizing it, and I felt as if a fire had been ignited. Slowly, she turned to face me. My fingers grazed her belly and brushed against a tiny mound, protected only by one or two layers of fine material. Through the black lace netting and the tips of her hat pins, the ambiguous woman smiled.

"Let's do it my way," she said.

She made me sit down and raised her skirt as she settled on my thighs, her back to me. My turgid stylus then entered a warm nook, and we began to rock in unison and she cried out as I massaged her breasts through the material of her dress or clung to the tender flesh of her ass. I had wanted her so much that it was hard to believe I was actually making love to her.

Only when she was gone did I begin to make certain connections and consider the possibility that she was, in fact, a transvestite. I would recall the shape of her breasts . . . perhaps just a bit too high, a bit too hard, to be real, and the backward position and the narrow orifice through which I had come. But my senses had not been conditioned to realize any of this, and after all, many women like to have sex Greek-style.

Bordeaux was liberated on September 2, 1944. And after that unsettling sexual encounter, the ambiguous woman never visited me again.

XVII

Games with Masks

For me, the postwar period was a period of rediscovery, of learning new techniques and painting styles. In an attempt to recreate my confiscated paintings I created frescos on two walls of my living room and perhaps because I didn't use enough sand for the paint mixture, they eventually deteriorated. In *Succubus,* the diabolical women hovering above the sleeping figures became a mottled stain. In *The Warrior Women,* the foot that the *Sud-Ouest* critic claimed was the best element of the entire painting slowly disintegrated. I didn't really care, though, as the foot in the mural didn't look much like the one in the canvas.

One evening, as I was primping for one of my profane rituals, I noticed a greenish-gray stain beneath one of my cheekbones, about the size of a mistletoe berry. It was no temporary discoloration, either; it was a blemish that was now a part of me, like my teeth, the color of my eyes, or the furrow between my eyebrows. As I covered it with a bit of powder, I thought about how this ritual of making up my face was equal parts coquetry and painterly skill. And although ordinarily this ritual was more than enough to arouse me, I realized that it would not always be able to hide the deterioration of the flesh. And, now, to think that was almost thirty years ago . . .

And so I turned to masks. Not the paper kind, for they are too hard and you can't kiss while wearing them, but masks that I could cut and shape myself, ones that were as soft to the touch as human skin.

In search of flexibility and fine texture, I tried various different animal skins—Moroccan leather, baby calfskin, sheepskin. I became an expert at picking out specific types of leather, tanning them, stretching them, varnishing them with lacquer, and polishing them to a shine. When I was finished, I would apply a coat of makeup that almost never needed retouching, and then I would place it on my face, which would be transformed into a face two, even three decades younger within seconds. Then I would match each mask with a wig and add a pair of pierced earrings, preferably the long, dangling kind. I still have most of the masks I made, and I am always pleased to see the seductive powers they still possess. Yet when I put them on, I have trouble finding the lovers that I used to be able to find inside of me. The trouble, and I know this all too well, is me, of course, and not the masks. But I still feel desire, such great desire. . . .

It was around that time that I decided to return to photography as a way of capturing the ephemeral. I began by teaching myself how to use light, how to isolate an image, how to create mystery. I would take photograph after photograph of myself dressed up as a woman, constantly changing accessories and adopting different poses, either in the mirrored room or beneath the glass ceiling in my studio. Then I learned developing and printing techniques, using my bathroom as a darkroom. I didn't have an enlarger, so I took an old wooden frame that I had built, and placed the negatives inside it. I would dry my prints on my clothesline, and as I hung them in their natural sequence I would relive the dizzying moments I had captured. Whenever I had managed to capture myself precisely at the moment of ejaculation, I would be so overwhelmed by the potency of the image that I would come once again while admiring it.

One day, as I stood in front of the window of a corset shop where the latest crop of lace-cup brassieres and nylon stockings with silken flecks were on display, I noticed a young woman watching me. I stared back at her, and though she grew flustered, she nonetheless followed me home. I could hardly believe that at my age I had made such a conquest. I opened the door to my building and turned toward her. She had green eyes that seemed to express every subtlety imaginable: reticence, concern, even compassion, and then irony and innocence, all at the same time. The refined summer dress she wore, with little yellow sunflower designs, accentuated her slim figure.

"I'm Muriel, Daddy," she said, offering me her hand.

My legs began to tremble. Like an idiot I asked her how old she was. Seventeen, she said. She seemed older to me, and yet at the same time I couldn't believe that so much time had passed since my separation from Lucie.

For a long while we stood there looking at each other in silence, as if we felt that only our eyes could be trusted at that moment; that words would force us to lie.

A motorcycle sped by, barely grazing us, making a loud noise. I think that was what made us go inside. With an exquisitely elastic stride she climbed the stairs ahead of me. Once inside my apartment I showed her my murals, my studio. Several shots of me, in mask and in character, were tacked to a corkboard. She blushed when she first saw them but quickly regained her composure and asked me who the model was. I told her the truth. She gazed at me, with an amused, slightly saucy look on her face, and I realized that unlike her mother, she was not easily shocked.

She told me she had just passed her final examinations at school, and that she wanted to study Egyptology in Paris, where she would live with one of her uncles. She had found my address and had been on the verge of visiting me several times, but she hadn't been allowed to walk through the city alone until very recently. Lucie, I deduced, must have been afraid that Muriel might find me one day. That morning, Muriel had walked down my street, unsure of whether to come upstairs. She had seen me leave the building and, realizing who I was, followed me as I did my shopping.

She didn't stay long that day, but she returned often. It was as if she needed to take our relationship in little doses, one step at a time. She loved the way I encouraged her femininity, and one day she let me do her makeup: I did her lips, eyebrows, eyelids. As she looked at herself, she was astonished at the transformation; never before had she seen herself so lovely. Some time later, she confided to me that as she left my house, she noticed how people looked at her in a different way. Her mother kissed her as if she suspected something and told her she smelled of men.

She asked me to take her photograph. She was anxious to continue this metamorphosis and also was eager to strengthen the ties between us. I was clearly playing with an advantage but I was unable to hold back and deny myself such intoxicating delights. Like a greedy procuress, I showed her all the tricks of seduction. I photographed her in street clothes as well as with some more suggestive accoutrements from my armoire. I was inspired and she was a fast learner. When she left, I waved my magic wand across her figure, barely concealed by a negligee left half-open to reveal the length of her leg.

I was so fearful of desiring her that I closed the web I had laid around her. I convinced myself that Muriel needed me, that she had spent years looking for a teacher, a shaman, someone who could not only bring out her essence, but truly revel in it as well. Who could caress her more tenderly, more affectionately than her own father?

One day I put on a mask. I asked Muriel to take off her panties and she hurriedly removed them as if she wanted to actively participate and not just passively submit herself to her deflowering. I gathered her in my arms and with almost no effort at all, carried her into the bedroom. To think that I might have died without ever having seen my daughter's cunt, that lush frond, that sweet little crevice. Once we were in, all the caresses I wanted to lavish upon her seemed superfluous somehow; I sensed that everything should be as simple and direct as possible, because making love to my daughter was like making love to myself.

I entered her rapidly, easily. Muriel exhaled in a moan that sounded like a lullaby and then she seemed to faint. Or perhaps she fell asleep. When she came to she told me that she had come, intensely and exquisitely.

That was the second time I went to bed with a virgin. The first time had been with her mother.

At the end of the summer, Muriel left for Paris.

XIX

The Little Vampire

Now that I had more than half a century behind me, the general lack of recognition for my work had begun to weigh heavily on me. In Bordeaux I was considered among the "undesirables." My house had acquired the kind of ill repute normally reserved for crime scenes, and my own neighbors would not even deign to say hello as they passed by me on the stairs. I wrote to Malraux, asking for his support to show some of my work in Paris. But Malraux, veteran editor of underground erotic literature, an adventurer who had sought riches by sacking the temples of Angkor, replied that he could not possibly pressure the Salon de Mai jury, and that I shouldn't count on his support, as it would conflict with his involvement in the Réunion des Musées Nationaux.

I then turned to Breton, and sent him a letter along with a folder filled with photographs of my more representative paintings. In the letter I explained the woeful situation I found myself in. On the letterhead of L'Étoile Scellé, his gallery, he replied that he was astounded by my work and that he would put his gallery at my disposal. He advised me to search my own paintings and imbue myself in their mastery, for that was how I would find the strength necessary to endure the disdain of the public. "I believe," he added, "that the days when contemporary artists were expected to behave like conformists are finally behind us."

In anticipation of the exhibition I sent him more photographs of my paintings, along with two canvases: *Stellar Breasts* and *The Veiled Women*. In his reply he confessed that he had become so enamored of my paintings that he had temporarily hung them in his own home. Due to a series of previous commitments, his gallery would not be free until 1956. I had just over a year to prepare the coup de grace that was to capture the public's attention.

It is odd to think of how terribly hard we try to earn the approval of people we don't even know, people who we would run from in any other circumstance. Little by little I developed a series of paintings, giving full rein to my most liberal appetites. Female bodies grew deformed and giant, recombining and then reducing down to nothing more than a thigh that opened onto a perfect breast, bypassing the notion of a belly entirely. Or they would become an inextricable maelstrom of disproportionate mouths, multiple asses, and feet as slender and sinuous as lips. In any spot at all, one might find a flaming vulva, and any part of the body was fair game for making love or for entering another body. A foot would slice into a thigh, a breast would pierce a belly. High-heeled shoes sparkled with precious stones that glistened against galactic, spermatic backgrounds and long, thick manes of hair.

Such a large amount of painting involved a torrent of semen which I mixed with my oils and also used as a varnish. My lover at the time, who doubled as my model, was a bar waitress whom I nicknamed "the little vampire," partially because of her size and partially because of her habit of nibbling ferociously at my neck as we made love, often drawing blood. My neck would be covered with bloody marks that took weeks to heal, but the sensation of risk—occasionally she told me she had to struggle not to bite through my flesh entirely—mysteriously heightened the pleasure I felt. With her sharply filed nails my little vampire would scratch and pinch my nipples, already highly sensitive from my frequent use of the gold rings Danielle had given me. In addition to all this, she seemed endlessly fascinated, even obsessed, by my hairless legs, and she would often stroke them for hours at a time. She was hardly conventional as a lover, and perhaps even dangerous, but she was absolutely habit-forming.

Once I arrived in Paris, I realized the gallery was too small to display the twenty-six paintings and fourteen drawings I had selected. Breton insisted that the drawings would sell better, so I eliminated some of the canvases. The gallery published a catalogue that contained a photograph of me in the nude, pointing a gun and bearing the title, "Three passions: painting, women, and weapons." In his introduction Breton compared me to Gustave Moreau and Edvard Munch and declared that my greatest achievement was my transformation of the female image, traditionally such a relegated figure. He declared I had turned it into something detonating, explosive, and frightening.

There was a rarefied air in the L'Étoile Scellé the night of the opening. Several renowned surrealists attended, and they treated me like one of their own. Breton, with his chilly gaze and masklike face, which almost never relaxed into a smile, said a few words and then closely examined every one of the works on display as if he had never seen them before. His acolytes, who gathered round my pieces in little groups, looked like a congregation of dirty old men peeking out of a brothel window.

In the days that followed, news of my work appeared in the local newspapers. The critics seemed disconcerted, and the general impression was that my paintings weren't terribly interesting for someone who had waited so long to finally exhibit them. When the show closed after a month and a half, I had only sold eleven drawings and six paintings. Breton felt this was a solid response, but I knew I had to resign myself to the fact that I would not achieve the apotheosis I had dreamed of. I would have to accept the sad evidence that

I must continue my work on my own. This time, I couldn't even console myself by saying that nobody had given me a chance. I had been judged, and they had chosen to ignore me.

It was a disillusioning trip in other ways as well. I didn't dare try to track down my daughter, for fear she might not want to see me. Danielle was no longer at her old address; the woman who looked after the building told me that she had gotten married, a most unexpected bit of news. And Madame Ulianov's brothel was gone as well. Peering through the metal grille that now covered the door and the windows, I could make out the figures of the pale white mannequins with their blond hair. Those ancient girls made of plaster and hemp were now coated with a thin film of dust; only their eyes still retained the sparkle of eternal life.

In 1960 I participated in the International Surrealist Exhibition with a pair of paintings that were accepted with a certain measure of reserve. But the following year, when I tried to contribute my *Masturbation of the Virgin Mary,* I didn't even receive a response. Clearly, the blasphemous nature of its content made it a difficult painting to accept for display. By then, my relationship with Breton and the surrealists had grown cold, something that in retrospect was not terribly surprising. I agreed with the surrealists' disdain for tradition, order, and convention, but their theories and general petulance bored me. And with the passage of time, they too had become an institution in their own way. And Breton and I had our differences: he was a champion of courtly love—a notion that did not reject carnal desire, but certainly didn't require it, either— whereas I have never been fully able to separate eroticism from sex. There was a moment when this became much more evident in my paintings. In the end, I think my obsession with sex made him uncomfortable; I think he simply found it vulgar.

One more ray of hope flashed through my life around that time: Raymond Borde, the music critic for *Les Temps Modernes,* decided to make a documentary about my odd little personal universe, and he filmed it in my home. The opening scene of *The Painter of Women* is sublime: all my paintings and fetishes captured beneath the flickering light of a flashlight, as if a thief had come to prey upon me in the night. Following that is an image of me firing my revolver at a porcelain Virgin Mary. One of the best takes is a traveling shot moving toward a totally motionless young woman who seems to be made of wax, until her face suddenly breaks into a smile. The young woman is played by my very own little vampire, who I had made up to look like a little doll. In another sequence, which was cut from the final version, I am captured lying in my funeral bed in a dark suit. A hand with long nails holds my erect member, which peeks out from the open zipper of my trousers. The documentary ends with the image of two women in corsets, stockings, and high heels, making love in the mirrored room.

The Virgin Mary sequence presented a few problems, and it was censored in some places. Nevertheless, the uncut version was shown for an entire week in a movie theater on the street where I live, along with *Un chien andalou.* The little vampire, however, never saw it, for she died in a car accident while it was being edited.

XX

The Plaster Venus

When I received the telegram from the château caretaker informing me that my mother had died, I wrote him back immediately, saying I was terribly sorry but I wouldn't be able to attend the burial. I sent him the address of one of her brothers who I was sure would take care of the ceremony. I did, however, promise him that I would visit the château sometime soon. The reason for my rebuff was not heartlessness; the affection I felt for my mother hadn't changed, but I wanted to remember her as she had been so long before, not as she was when she died. And I didn't want to feel guilty, either. Death, I think, is much easier to face when you are either very young or very old, not when you see yourself as middle-aged and suddenly realize that you only have one or two decades left to live. I had already begun to add seven or eight years to my age whenever I spoke of these things with strangers, just to feel the pleasure of someone saying, "Really? That can't be possible! You don't look your age at all!"

The day I arrived, I sent my luggage ahead of me and walked along the riverbank for several hours, just like that afternoon when I walked the same path to avoid going back home and facing my mother, the day after I had made love to her. I saw no boats or loons this time, and the old country lanes were now paved with asphalt. Through the sheath of clouds the sun shone down in thin slivers of light.

At the château everything was the same, except for the wine production area, which had been expanded considerably and which now housed a manufacturing plant. The servants, none of whom I knew, greeted me skeptically. I ate my dinner, though I had little appetite, and went to sleep in my old room.

As I slept, from some place in the past, I heard my own voice calling out, "Sophie . . . Justine . . . Justine . . . Nicole . . . Nicole . . . !"

"Oh, Sir!" Anne-Marie exclaimed, suddenly entering my bedroom. "This explains so many things, Monsieur Pierre. Would you like me to help?"

"I'd like that very much."

"Put your hand between my legs. Does that feel good?" she asked me sweetly.

"Oh yes, so good. It's so warm, so wet . . ."

In the celerity of dreams, Anne-Marie suddenly became my sister Muriel, who fondled one of her breasts as she removed one of her smooth slippers, and then, with heartrending tenderness, rested the sole of her foot on the most sensitive part of my body.

"Even through your pants," she said, "I can feel it, strong and hard."

"Anne-Marie . . . Muriel!" I cried into the darkness. "Mother!" I shouted, stretching out my arms.

"She's dead, Pierre," the singsong voice of Tutune reminded me.

I woke up in anguish, with a mediocre erection. I searched for the oil lamp that was no longer there, and instead my hand found a light switch.

In robe and slippers I raced down the corridors to my mother's room. I stopped in front of the door, gathered my strength, and turned the knob, to no avail. It occurred to me that maybe she wasn't dead after all, that the caretaker's telegram had only been a decoy to lure me to the château. Then I told myself that I shouldn't be surprised that the door to her room was locked.

The door to the library, on the other hand, opened easily. Some understanding soul must have known that I might need to go inside, and had left the door open. With gratitude and relief I went through the books I knew so well, caressing their bindings. I thought of all the time they had spent there, lining those bookshelves, educating and intoxicating future generations of readers. I thought of the second Muriel, who would inherit all this one day, and I wondered if she had married. Perhaps I was a grandfather and didn't even know it. Perhaps my granddaughter possessed, or would possess, a beautiful pair of legs. I pulled out the *Anti-Justine* thinking the book that had helped me endure my father's death could help alleviate my pain this time. I searched for sections I knew and found that they were as effective as ever.

The next day I asked for the key to my mother's bedroom. It calmed me to be in her room. I stood there staring at her bed for a long while, remembering conversations and imagining new ones that would never take place. Then I began to rifle through her things, though without much hope of finding anything. In the bottom drawer of one of her dressers, however, I found a few pieces of the lingerie that had inflamed me so many years earlier, but which now seemed oddly innocent. Only the champagne-colored corset still shone in its own light, and it was as thrilling as I remembered it. In a corner of her dressing room I also found some of the shoes she had worn when she was younger. I don't know why she had saved those things. Perhaps they helped her to relive the past, just as the books had done for me, or perhaps they helped her stave off the passage of time. Perhaps, before dying, she had tried on those tidbits and gazed at herself in the mirror to see how they looked. Perhaps she was like me. I grabbed the corset and a pair of shoes covered in black feathers and left the sanctuary.

I had to speak with the caretaker, the lawyer, and the manager of the wine operation. They brought me up to date on things: we had no debts, I was the only heir, and the projections for our wine business were still good. I could continue to get by on what the angels lived on without having to sell any of our property. In between the many reports I had to read I would relax with a bit of target practice, aiming my old revolver at the trees in the countryside, like an idle country gentleman.

Pigeons now nested in the tower where years before I had thought I had seen signs of my mother's betrayal. I went through all the old trunks, admiring the weapons and uniforms that had belonged to my remote ancestor. At the foot of the window, on that wide windowsill, a pair of slender hands had left their mark in the dust so long ago. My eyes were once again drawn to the odd contour of the windowsill. I went out and came back with a club and broke through the false brick ledge. Inside I found a wooden box that contained a diary and some photographs of my father as a young man, making love to a plaster of paris Venus. In the diary my father explained how he had found the Venus one day in an art-supply shop and bought it immediately. For the next three years he had become a slave to that idol, reveling in it in various different ways. I imagine the relationship was aborted when he met the beautiful Polish woman. In one of the photographs, the Venus wore a fur coat; in another, a tight leather bandage.

No mention was made in the diary about the fate of that statue, but I now had the vague recollection of having seen it as a very young boy, and if nobody had destroyed it, there was only one place it could be. I forced open the other tower and there it was, hidden beneath a dusty canvas dropcloth: a white, radiant Venus with lips half-parted in a soft smile, resting the weight of her body on her right leg, with her left leg bent as if she were about to take a step forward. I felt an erotic rumble inside of me, the same rumble my father must have felt as he spied her in that art-supply store, the same rumble that Madame Ulianov's clients must have felt as they gazed into her windows at the mannequins whose look always changed with the times. And perhaps it was the same erotic rumble I had felt right there as a child the very first time I ever visited the tower on that busy day when I joined the servants as they put furniture into storage. It was the same erotic rumble that all women and mannequins with long legs inspire in me.

My mother was buried next to my father in the little cemetery at Léognan. Her presence in the house was still so intense that it seemed superfluous to actually go to the gravesite. Before returning to Bordeaux, however, I had the nerve to plant a black cross at the far end of the garden, with my name and with this long inscription in white letters: "Born April 13, 1900. Died on an unimportant day. Was a slave to the beauty of women. Utterly lacking in morality. Do not even bother praying for him."

XXI

The Mummies

I liked to think that my premature burial represented my death to the world, to the bourgeois society that rejected me and that I provoked at every possible opportunity. I no longer minded masturbating before my visitors as we chatted away in my house, and I did the same thing in broad daylight, in front of all the women that appealed to me, in the outdoor terraces of the cafés and in parks. Nor did I mind it when the police would arrest me for indecent behavior, which they did a few times, just as they had done before, during the Three Graces scandal. What society considered my worst vices I regarded as my most fervent passions.

For my own pleasure I crafted a set of vibrators, infinitely flexible and with a perfect satin sheen, with long, thin, fine leather straps braided and covered in the softest materials. I would place a condom over these gadgets and sodomize myself with them. I made them in a myriad of shapes and colors, and even created a queen-sized version. In order to free my hands I took a pair of women's shoes and tied the quasi-manly monstrosity to one of the heels so that it stuck out like the talon of a bird of prey.

All I had to do was either straddle it directly or lie on my side in bed and bend my leg back, with my foot in the newly-outfitted shoe.

I had a hunch that this self-sodomization would be infinitely more pleasurable if I first administered an enema to relax the tight orifice, and then did it in the presence of my many mirrors. Whenever I wanted to impress or shock people, I would send them a photograph in which they could admire my high heels, my legs encased in a pair of stockings, my ass in the throes of a sodomizing rapture, and with a translucent slip of fabric wrapped around my testicles to hide them from view. I still laugh at the thought that more than one person must have masturbated away at the sight of those images; I can just picture them reaching the heights of ecstasy before that remarkably feminine ass.

Tying up a woman requires a healthy imagination as well as a high degree of mental concentration. You have to be every bit as alert as your "victim," for she is the one who controls the situation, not you. You have to predict her fears and justify them, and you have to know that when she closes her eyes it is because she wants to be blindfolded, and that when she threatens to scream she does so because she wants you to bite into her flesh. I have never denied any lover these satisfactions. I would tie her wrists behind her back and then place a thick cord above one shoulder, below one breast, and then above the other shoulder. Then I would slip it between her legs, nice and tight, bind her ankles together, and then finish it off by wrapping the cord around her waist and belly. The cord pressing against her skin would create a jagged indentation, which was as stimulating as the spectacle she created by fighting against the ties that bound her. The cord around her legs forced the lips of her vagina wide open, and all you had to do was push it up toward her inner thigh to delicately graze her rosy button.

There was one diversion, a far less common one, that none of the women had ever tried until they met me: it involved wrapping them up entirely, either with several layers of sheets or with a very long strip of gauze bandage. The tightly wrapped material or clinging bandage transformed a voluptuous body into an irresistible, perfect intumescence. And the faces without features acquired a mysterious appeal, like blocks of unsculpted marble. All you had was the white relief of the woman you so desired. I called it "playing mummies." One particular call-girl always charged me more for playing that game because it suffocated her so. And when they did the same to me, the part I liked the most was when they would wrap up my penis.

If I wasn't in the mood to talk to anyone, I would turn to mannequins instead of women. I had several in my house; most of them were made of a light polyester fiber, a pliant material that I could shape and mold as I wished. I would part their legs and line their crevices with silk. This would be my field of action.

In bed, the bottom half of a soft mannequin would serve as my companion. I would introduce my rigid member between her ass cheeks, reveling in the exquisitely painted face of one of my masks. It wasn't like being with a woman, of course, because there was no movement, no life. But it did have a certain charm. You could lie there and just fantasize away that you were desecrating a beautiful, dismembered corpse.

I began to create photomontages because untouched photographs simply couldn't capture the motley combination of ghosts in my mind. The vision of a mannequin's head above a real woman's body, or my masked face above a mannequin dressed up in my favorite clothes, aroused me far more than the mannequin, the woman, or myself alone.

This ritual allowed me to select the most appealing aspects of the women I knew, take them apart, and rearrange them to form my own version of the ideal woman. The result was almost always a rather motley assemblage of the fragmented bits I would gather: the breasts of one woman with the hips of another and the legs of a third. I was also able to achieve a mirror effect, just as I had done in my paintings, creating extravagant creatures with several asses, perched upon a mountain of legs and feet.

Unlike my paintings or my drawings, my photomontages required advance preparation, as I had to locate the physical objects I would be photographing. I would print the images, retouch the original negative with a charcoal pencil, and then I would print them again. At that point I would begin the painstaking editing process: the montage of the various body parts, then photographing the montage, then retouching the new negative until I achieved the perfect image. I would spend days drawing veils, fishnets, and suggestively-patterned lace on my mannequins' skin in the negatives, either to soften or sharpen the contrasts.

All of this led me to put together a book of sixty-nine photomontages that I wanted to call "The Shaman and His Disciples." It had to be a flawlessly printed book, an object of beauty, unusual and coveted by bibliophiles. But my technical demands coupled with the financial limitations of the four publishers I approached made it all but impossible. If someone ever decides to take up the cause after my death but fails to carefully follow the directions that accompany the prototype of the book that sits on my desk, I can promise that the most vulgar part of my body—which I fervently believe will far outlive my spirit—will abandon the infinite pleasures of hell to come back and torment him or her.

XXII

The Priestess of Love

The L'Intendance bookstore, Bordeaux's meeting place for the intellectual periphery, was where I first opened a copy of *Arianne,* the erotic novel that had been on the bestseller lists in France for two years. Its tremendous success had made me skeptical, and until then I had never deigned to look at it. But now I found myself reading a scene in which a woman received her lover's ecstasy in her mouth, perched her lips on the open sex of another woman, and then filled it with sperm. I was enraptured by the words of that fantastically lewd tale, and I knew I had found my soulmate, someone passionate about eroticism, someone like me, who cared more about the contours of flesh than the convictions of contemporary conventions.

Arianne de Saynes was no doubt a pseudonym. I had to do quite a bit of persuading to get her publisher to give me her real name and address. At the time, Marayat Mérogis was living in Bangkok, where her husband worked for an international organization of some sort. I sent her an album with photomontages and photographs of my paintings. She wrote back almost immediately. Upon seeing my samples she too had felt a bond, intimate and powerful, drawing us together. "I adore your paintings," she wrote to me. "They are the only paintings I wish I could have created myself. I identify with all your women: those who embrace each other, caress each other, open their legs and penetrate each other. I am their eyes, their lips, their breasts, and their sex. And I am the woman who feasts on them. I am you just as I am me, and I am you without ever having laid eyes on you, without knowing anything about you."

I answered her immediately, and she responded: "What Arianne has written, you have painted. The orgasm in your work is the same one that I have felt. Finally I know I am not alone. You are my other me, my double, the missing half of the elemental androgyny that we were at some other time."

She attached a photograph of her face: a young, very distinguished-looking woman with long black hair, half-open mouth, and prominently arched eyebrows that framed her large, slanted eyes, almond-shaped and extending to the edges of her temples. Such beauty seemed anathema to the notion of makeup, but I knew very well how many hours it took in front of a vanity mirror to achieve such a convincing imitation of nature. That was when I experienced something that felt like love, even if it wasn't. Even from such a long distance away, it was an intense, physical love. I masturbated with determination, imagining those almond eyes were gazing at me, and that perhaps she, thousands of miles away, was caressing herself at the very same moment.

In our letters we were neither bashful nor prudish. We shared with each other all our personal ghosts, immersing ourselves in the excesses of fiction and words. Our letters even began to sound the same, and sometimes I wasn't sure if her words were meant for me or if they were part of a chapter of one of her novels. And I wasn't terribly certain myself whether what I wrote was fiction or reality. When she wrote to tell me that she would soon be coming to Paris and that we could finally meet, I began to have trouble sleeping.

Despite the fact that her photograph and her books suggested otherwise, I was somehow expecting an Asian woman with coral earrings, link bracelets, and toe rings. Instead I found myself before a woman in sunglasses, patent leather sandals, a white dress with wide lapels, V-neck, and A-line skirt, and a belt with a round buckle. It was a reserved, elegant look, refined and understated. But when she removed the glasses and I saw in her eyes the same intense passion and beauty that I found in her writing, I realized I was not wrong to have thought of myself as the physical lover of Arianne (or Marayat, as I preferred calling her) even before I ever saw her in the flesh. We met. We spoke about painting, about erotica. She was with her husband, and they were in a bit of a rush. I gave them one of my paintings, *The Arrow of Love,* and three homemade vibrators of different sizes and calibrations.

"I am full of wild happiness, admiration, and gratitude," she wrote upon her return to Bangkok. "I didn't send word sooner only because I am spending most of my time making love with your marvelous devices. All three have shown an impressive level of performance and craftsmanship. It is as if they were made specifically to survive inside of my thick, burning lava. I switch from one to the other so frequently that I no longer know which is responsible for my most intense moments of pleasure. Your painting sits before me always, inspiring me and compelling me to repeat the ritual of ecstasy."

My letters were no less passionate. We reveled in our mutual bliss, and in the fantasy that I was her double and she was mine, both of us feeling that we knew each other so well it was as if we had been making love since the tendrils of childhood had begun to grow inside our minds, filling them up like abundantly flowering tumbleweed. I clung to her confessions like a drug addict would his daily dose, and when a day would go by without a letter from her, it would feel like failure. She felt exactly the same. And as we shared the depths of pain to which we brought each other, we would once again feel our mutual ecstasy. After about a year or so of this explosive correspondence, we were almost suffocating from the staggering amount of fuel we had thrown to the fire we had lit together. That was when Marayat wrote to tell me that she would be coming to Bordeaux for a night.

I don't know how but I knew her visit would be something we would never repeat. In honor of my beloved I polished the vibrators, touched up the makeup on the masks, and moved my bed into the mirrored room.

She came to my house straight from the station. I took photographs of her in the nude, standing in front of my paintings, surrounded by mannequins, her face hidden by various masks. I removed my clothes but found I couldn't bring myself to touch her, because her body was so very ravishing; its symmetry and proportions far exceeded anything I had ever seen before. I began to stroke myself, brandishing my penis like an animal in heat. I felt an odd kind of modesty yet at the same time, a kind of arrogant lust.

Marayat's fingers settled on her prominent vulva, easily locating the fissure between the two fleshy flaps, and from there they descended down toward her ass in a hypnotic circular motion. Suddenly, like a beetle opening its wings, her thumb left its nook next to the other four fingers and began to bury itself deeper and deeper as she rocked her body round and round, back and forth, her knees pressed tightly together. This priestess of love was offering herself to herself. She said one word only:

"Come!"

Fluttering clumsily, my penis searched for her in the dark. We were soon locked in the kiss of magnet and needle, and as we slowly inched closer and closer, the mirrored ceiling and walls became a forest of different people, where ten different women made love to ten different men all at once.

We fell onto the bed. She helped me plunge inside her and I felt as though she were sucking me, as if she were trying to extract my nectar with all the powers of her belly and ass. I wanted Marayat to come first, and I stabbed her with the full length and thickness of my penis. She screamed, which aroused me even more, and soon I was crying out as well, in a hoarse, frighteningly inhuman voice, as she flailed left and right as if being flagellated. After a little while, her ecstasy subsided, and as she rested against my cheek she began to purr, letting out little sobs.

"Wait," she said after a short while, when she felt my body reawaken with arousal. "I brought you something."

She got up and returned with a gold ring just big enough to fit on my pinky finger, with an encrusted ruby and our names engraved on the surface.

Some time before I had built a set of double vibrators to photograph two women making love with them, but I had never asked anyone to sodomize me with them. I showed them to Marayat and asked her to pick one. She nodded knowingly and took the larger of the two. With a sigh, she inserted it in her warm nest. I knelt down, my back to her, and the tip of the vibrator that jutted out from her body moved forward steadily into my ass. As the close-cut mat of her pubic hair brushed against my skin, Marayat thoughtfully refrained from moving in and out, knowing that I still felt that initial bit of pain. She held back, only allowing the vibrator to rotate slightly as it brought moans to her lips and strained the limits of my internal tissues. Then, like a man who had endured the torture of chastity for years, she released all her fury.

We made love almost all through the night; I felt every bit as robust and virile as I had been years earlier, and when dawn broke I fell asleep with a tremendous sensation of clarity and peace. Glistening stalactites peeped out of her warm little cave.

"This," I said to her as I closed my eyes, "was like making love with all the creatures in my paintings."

When I awoke, she was gone. It was around noontime. There was a long note on the table:

"My obsession for you has often felt like a sickness, like a fever that exhausts and depletes yet at the same time invigorates all my faculties. I was afraid that we would reach a moment in which I would have to consecrate myself to you, and this made me frightened because I have always felt that truly loving behavior—and as such that of a woman who wants to fulfill that notion—calls for shared experience in an open, evolved society, not in a small group or within a closed couple absorbed in one another. I wanted to avoid that situation, free myself from you. But I couldn't do that without giving myself up to you first. It wouldn't have been honest for either of us. I even secretly hoped that you would disappoint me somehow, that you would prove unworthy of my adoration and reverence. But that didn't happen: our night together was the most beautiful, thrilling night of my entire life. Suddenly you were absolutely timeless. You had no age, and you were neither an animal nor a creature from another planet nor a man. Perhaps you were a demigod. I had never seen anyone come so abundantly as you did. We have surpassed all of our desires. And by giving myself to you, possessing you as you wanted me to, I have gained all that I need to return and find my way, on my own."

I wrote back to her a few times, but never received any response. I know that she and her husband moved to Rome. I never saw her again, but that face with those almond-shaped eyes and that long black hair have found their way into some of my paintings, and in my photomontages her legs and amber breasts glow brightly between the bodies of other women and the lightweight polyester of my mannequins.

XXIII

The Woman with the Fetish

Breton always insisted that true love could not be felt for more than one woman. But when you reminded him that he had been married three times and had had plenty of lovers, he would argue testily that multiple love affairs helped a man more clearly define his image of the ideal woman, and that one's last lover was the result of an entire lifetime of searching. This was how I felt about Sieglinde. I suppose that as one approaches the end it is rather normal to think that everything has a meaning, that all the pieces should fit together in some way.

The sudden end of my relationship with Marayat either caused or coincided with a sharp decline in my health. Like those people from tropical islands who fall desperately ill from a flu epidemic, I found myself debilitated and virtually destroyed by a combination of different ailments that suddenly rendered me an old man—gallstones, liver problems, rheumatism. For the first time in my life I thought about suicide. My doctors attributed it all to nerves, but they didn't want to take any risks and advised me to have my gall bladder removed. Six months after the operation, the pain returned. I couldn't concentrate on anything at all—even painting no longer appealed to me.

One day a young woman came to the house. Tall, blond, and dressed in black, she had a sporty, clean air about her and looked at me with almost transparent eyes as she handed me a letter of introduction from Rainer Gruber, a German man who taught art and visual communication at the University of Giessen and with whom I had maintained a lengthy correspondence regarding the omnipresent eroticism of my paintings. In the letter, Rainer said that Sieglinde might be a liaison between the two of us. She was his lover, and he said that she and I had similar tastes.

I thought he was referring to painting. But when I asked Sieglinde about these particular tastes she took her dress off and paraded about before me from one end of the salon to the other, and she did this with a studied ease and an amused haughtiness that I only understood afterward, when I found out that in addition to studying at the École des Beaux-Arts in Paris, she had worked as a model for Christian Dior. She wore a black corset open in front with a little string that dangled from her breasts down to her belly, and her floral-motif garter and lace-and-satin panties revealed a healthy portion of ass. The black stockings she wore drew my attention to a pair of very long legs, unusually slender at the knees and calves. In the sacred diamond formed by the straps of her garter belt and the V of her inner thigh, slick curls peeked through her transparent panties. As if by magic, all my aches and pains vanished and my old, lusty friend grew hard again. Sieglinde smiled serenely, as if inviting me to interrupt her show. But as I sat before such a dazzling vision I was not so sure I wanted to make it disappear. Sieglinde sensed my sudden indecision, turned around a couple of times, and sat down.

"Don't you like it?" she asked me in her strong accent.

"You have brought me back to life. You are exquisite. But I don't know quite what I can give you."

"The big hand of the clock knows," she said with a smile, casting a glance down between my thighs. "It's almost noon, and I think it's ready to strike twelve."

Turning her back to me, she got up and walked toward the desk. Lowering her panties, she separated her legs and bent down, revealing the soft opening between her luscious ass cheeks. A moment later, my resuscitated instrument was pointing straight at her. I placed my hands beneath Sieglinde's corset, fondling her breasts as I pressed my belly against her ass and swayed back and forth. I felt a rush as her breasts hardened to my touch and was moved by the thought that at my age I was still able to evoke such tremors of pleasure.

Once we had both come and the arc of passion had subsided into a mellow afterglow, I led her to the mirrored room and together we fell asleep.

"The best lover," she said later, studying my skinny body, "is not necessarily the youngest, but the one with the most imagination."

"I'm afraid even that is beginning to fail me."

"Oh, but I'll help you," she assured me. And as if sensing my hesitation, she added: "I won't hurt you. We'll play as long as you want to and then we'll stop when you get tired."

"If you could have seen me twenty years ago. . . . But now I have a double chin, and even my underarms have wrinkles. My face is horrendous."

"I want to see you exactly as you are," she said. "I have my whims, too, you know."

She then told me that she had left her suitcase at the train station and I went with her to pick it up, for I was afraid of losing her too soon. Most of the space in her suitcase was taken up by a wide assortment of absolutely dazzling lingerie. In the weeks that followed, I would attend many, many of her intimate fashion shows.

One night she was jolted awake by acute menstrual pains and she couldn't fall back asleep. She lay there moaning until the early dawn hours, and I suffered as much as she did. It hurt me to think that her monthly period forced her to endure such a recurring, severe pain.

After a few days her condition improved, and she began to encourage me to return to my painting. I photographed and painted her image several times until the day she told me she had to go away. She would be going to

Paris, she said, and then to Giessen, where she would make love to Rainer and tell him about my paintings. When I asked her if it didn't feel rather strange to go from one lover to another like that, she replied that that was the most natural thing in the world, for women and men alike.

I wrote to her in Germany, thanking her for what she had done for me: "My darling, darling of all your lovers, I shower you with kisses. Since you left me I have not stopped working on your portraits. I found something that belonged to you, a tampon, that was inside you not so long ago, and I have carefully saved it so that I might hold on to something that retains the shape of your sex, like a tiny memento of you."

I didn't know if she would ever come back, but she did, not once but many times. And in all these twilight years, Sieglinde has been my muse, my rock. In addition to her lingerie exhibitions, she also loved to try on shoes for me. She would put them on and walk around a bit, showing them off from various different positions and angles, clicking her heels just like the heroines I read about in the books by Restif de la Bretonne, before taking them off and trying on another pair. On one occasion she rubbed her cloven mound against a black high-heeled shoe, which she then placed on her foot. She asked me to lick it, and began to masturbate as I licked and kissed the gleaming surface of the shoe. On the brink of orgasm she called out to me for help. My tongue raced from the shoe all the way up to her little pink threshold as I brought myself pleasure with my hands.

In the process she lost a spider-shaped earring that she loved, and later I found it mixed up in the sheets. She thanked me by making love to me for hours, and after that we played a little game of losing her earrings on purpose, and I would help her find them.

Sometimes we would get dressed up in costumes and masks—feathers for her, leather for me. She loved to take walks through the parks, especially through the magnolia trees in the public gardens. When we would go out at night, she would let me make her up and she would put on a long dress, with a voluminous black lace skirt, and a strapless bodice that revealed her shoulders. She was spectacular, and the faceless people we passed by in the streets were always dazzled at the sight of her.

One night we came across an orange-colored cat in the street, the reincarnation of Toulouse. Sieglinde decided to take it home. Now, she explained, I wouldn't have to be alone for the three or four months before her next visit. We brought him home and I named him d'Eon.

The next morning, I took her to the train station. Back at home, I put on a mask and tried to masturbate while gazing at myself in the mirror, but the old spell no longer worked. The photographs of Sieglinde, however, aroused me almost immediately and her image continued to inspire me for several days. I saved my semen and stored it in the refrigerator as always, planning to use it for my next painting session.

Then, about two weeks ago, I woke up to a paralyzing pain that shot through my back, my left arm, and hip. The pressure was almost unbearable; I felt as if I was about to break apart into little pieces. As if that wasn't enough, I began to feel pain in my gallbladder again, even though it had been removed. Medical tests revealed no clues as to the cause of this intense pain, but I knew what it was: the dead-end road of old age, and this made me infuriated and depressed.

I would never paint again. I would never make love again.

Almost forty years had gone by since my one and only literary effort, *Le Chevalier d'Eon*. But perhaps it wasn't too late to embark on a new project, this time in the company of all my ghosts. I stockpiled food, disconnected my doorbell, and began to write.

I'm worried about the cat, though. I can't help thinking about how frightened he will be when he hears the shot being fired.

XXIV

Final Encounter

I took my last walk the day before yesterday. I went to the public gardens that Sieglinde loved so much, and discovered that a large portion of the main avenue had been cut off for some supposed construction work. All that remains open is a long fenced-in stretch of sidewalk. I made my way through the narrow provisional walkway about two hundred meters long, tucked between the fences and the scaffold that surround the construction site.

Suddenly I spotted a woman walking toward me from the other end of the passageway. She must have entered at around the same time that I did from the other end. We looked at each other from afar, knowing that when we finally met, one of us would have to let the other by. I'm sure she thought for a second, just as I did, about turning around and taking another route. But instead she decided, just as I did, to continue on.

She was young and wore an ample, oyster-gray dress. I felt as if I knew her from somewhere, yet I couldn't quite place her face. As we approached each other I felt an increasingly violent sensation grow inside of me, and I knew that looking her in the face would only make both of us even more uncomfortable, given the circumstance.

At a certain moment, her feet became like two magnets that filled my entire field of vision. She moved forward slowly, oddly, lifting her sole and heel almost vertically, as if walking on tiptoe. Her shoes had extremely high heels and a tiny triangle of black leather that barely covered the tips of her toes. A few very thin strips ran down the length of her foot.

I slowed down as well, walking toward her in slow motion, as if trying to permanently etch in my memory every last detail of her feet bound up in those shoes. Then I moved to the right and slid by her, brushing against the fence. I didn't dare turn back, but the spellbinding thought of her exposed heels walking away from me raced through my mind.

When there was a fair distance between us, I felt a sudden urge and turned around, and at the very same moment she did, too. With an odd, gleeful delight I recognized the large eyes, the wide cheekbones, and the thick lips of the beautiful Polish woman, or perhaps it was her ghost. How could I not have recognized her, when almost seventy years earlier Anne-Marie had described the way she walked in such exquisite detail to my sister and me?

We stared at each other for several tense, expectant moments. I was about to follow her until I read in her face that that was what she was most frightened of. I didn't know her name. I didn't even know if she was a real woman, of real flesh and blood.

She did turn around one more time before disappearing down the far end of the passageway where I had entered.

I thought of the sexual act with her, what it would have been like. And of the impossibility of being together, and of lost opportunities. And of my ancient body. And of the naked finale of the beautiful foreign woman when she went on her last horseback ride. And of the eternal caress of her open vulva against the mane and lustrous saddle of her horse on that last night when she went looking for or running from something that we will never know, galloping away from Domaine de Chevalier toward the sea.

XXV
The Painted Nails

I have bequeathed my paintings to Sieglinde. This afternoon I sent a letter to the university's department of medicine, willing my body to science, then wrote another letter to the police, explaining that I have voluntarily chosen death. It was a necessary nuisance: I couldn't let some poor fool get arrested on my account.

Sometimes, after masturbation or sex, I would feel the episode slowly ebb, followed by the sensation that it could only be prolonged by another bout of ecstasy. Ever since I was eleven years old, whether living alone or in the company of a woman, I have always masturbated at least once a day. I wouldn't be able to fall asleep otherwise. I can no longer recall the number of women I've slept with, and I didn't always keep track of how many times I made love to each one.

Were those moments of complete pleasure the most important moments of my life? Are my paintings, my photomontages, even these words that I write, different techniques of prolonging my ecstasy? Is my lust, the lust of an old man, anything more than the longing to recapture the intoxicating sensations of adolescent desire?

When the Chevalier d'Eon died in 1810, the owner
of the pension he lived in declared the following: "I at-
test that the aforementioned gentleman has lived in my
home for approximately three years, during which time
I always believed him to be a woman, and today, having
seen his body after his death, I have discovered him to be
a man."

I, too, will leave a surprise behind. As if preparing
for the arrival of my lover, I have bathed, shaved, waxed,
and perfumed my body. I have made sure that the deep
red lacquer on my toenails is not chipped, and to complete
my outfit I have put my gold rings on my nipples, a lace
garter belt around my hips, and smoke-colored stockings
on my legs.

I am reminded of a novel by Octave Mirbeau in
which an old man dies while stroking a short boot recently
worn by his servant girl. What a weak finale for a man's
entire life. I, on the other hand, have chosen a far more
baroque approach: just like Delacroix's *Sardanapalus,* I
have rolled out my full collection of trinkets, icons, and
accoutrements: the photograph and the painting of my
sister on her death bed, my mother's champagne-colored
corset and feathered shoes, a nude portrait of Tutune, a
photograph of my daughter showing off her legs through
the opening of her negligee, the vibrator Marayat used
to sodomize me, the black heel that still exudes the aroma
of Sieglinde's sex. Photomontages of women's feet and
high-heeled sandals. Masks made of the finest leather,
mannequins in pleated satin brassieres, panties with deep

décolletage and tulle appliqués, corsets with little flounces peeking out from the bottom. And the revolver that will soon transform me into a work of fiction. And sitting on two chairs, propped against one wall of mirrors, the *Battle of the Amazons.*

My magic wand grows impatient. Dying in the throes of orgasm, surrounded by all my fetishes, I dream of the delectable arch of a woman's foot descending from high above and coming to rest upon my sex with all its might.